Barbados Heroine

I0520470

Sherwin A Goodman

Sherwin A Goodman

Barbados Heroine

Copyright © 2021   Sherwin A Goodman

ISBN:9781777103484

Barbados Heroine

Chapter 1

Monica Williams. A tall, beautiful brown skin woman with full luscious lips and short curly jet black hair and a lithe body. Wherever she went, men and women looked at her with envy, for not only was she beautiful, she was smart and a woman to be reckoned with, well educated, and street savvy.

~ ~ ~

At a young age, Monica and her sister Stephany and brother Theodore left Barbados with their parents Sybil Goodridge and Rosevelt Williams- and move to London, England, to live.

Rosevelt Williams, after arriving in London, UK. He worked for the London transport board driving buses. Rosevelt stayed in that job for three years, then went into business for himself and open a pub-restaurant and catering business.

~ ~ ~

Rosevelt expanded his business and opened three more establishments in various parts of London.

He catered to many exclusive events for the rich and famous as well as weddings, funerals and regular parties.

Having a function? Williams catering was the people you need to have taking care of the food and drinks for your event.

Sybil Goodridge/Williams went to school and took a nursing course, after graduating, Sybil took a job with the N.H.S of London.

But as her husband business grew, Sybil decided to take a night course in book keeping and money management. After receiving her diploma she gave up nursing and worked from home doing the

books of the family business and looking after

the children who were attending school.

~ ~ ~

During her time at Wanstead High School, all the students found out she wasn't to be crossed in anyway.

Monica didn't stand for nonsense from any of the students.

After high school, Monica studied computer science and literature at the University of London, and then business administration at the London School of Economics. After graduating, she took a job with the London exchange company.

"Why don't you go to Barbados and visit your family?" her father suggested after she returned from one of her vacation trips. "You have many relatives living there who would love to see you."

"I will, on my next vacation," she promised after returning from one of her trips to Cuba.

"Your mother and I still have a piece of real estate there, twelve acres, to be exact. We are thinking about selling it."

On her first visit to Barbados, Monica went alone and rented a room at a local guest house, leaving her fiance Joseph Gibbs in London because he couldn't get the time off from his job to travel with her.

She stayed for three weeks learning about her relatives and the habits of the Island, Monica also made inquiries on her parent's property and visited the area.

Two months after she returned from Barbados to London, her fiance was stab while crossing the Westminister Bridge, and he later died in the hospital from the wounds he sustained. His death devastated her.

Monica Uncle Otis, lives in Miami, Florida, he owns a beach house in Barbados, which he rents to visitors six months every year.

Otis, a successful business man founder and CEO of Williams Import and Export company.

Before marrying Alice Hernandez, Otis was a lover and frequent visitor to Vegas and did very well at the poker table.

He enjoyed visiting the city in the desert. What not to like he always say. Gambling, beautiful hot and sexy babes, some willing to do anything you asked of them.

Otis visits to the sin city went on for many years until one day as he was about to left the plane, a beautiful stewardess looked at him.

"I hope you win lots of money," the stewardess said to Otis.

"I hope so too," he replied while looking at her with a smile, he winked at her and got off the plane.

Barbados Heroine

Chapter 2

For his next flight to Vegas, Otis booked with the same airline and travel time, with the expectation of seeing the same stewardess again. He boarded the flight and took his seat in first class, and there she was, talking to a passenger two seats away.

"Did you win?"she asked when she reaches where Otis was seated.

"Yes, I did, and I owe it all to you, Alice."

"What's my percentage? 70/30?" she asked.

"I thinking more of 10 per cent Mrs Alice," Otis said kindly.

"It's Miss."

"Hi Miss Alice, I'm Otis Williams."

"Alice Hernandez, at your service," she replied.

"Nice to meet you Miss Alice Hernandez."

"Likewise Mr Otis Williams, enjoy your flight."

"Now that you're working on this flight, I know I will."

Alice gave Otis a warm towel and went along to the other passengers in first class.

Business dealings kept Otis away from his routine weekly visits to Vegas.

Three weeks later, Otis boarded the American Airlines flight heading for Las Vegas.

When he began to walk down the aisle heading for his seat, Alice Hernandez was walking towards him, her face light up with a smile from ear to ear.

"Hello, Miss Hernandez," Otis said when they meet face to face.

"Hello, yourself Mr. Williams," Alice responded. "Are you hiding from me?"

"No. Hide from you? No way, would love to see more of you," Otis said.

"We'll chat after departure," Alice promised.

During the flight when Alice made her rounds through the cabin taking drink orders, she handed Otis a note.

"Here's my number, I'll be expecting a call when you return to Miami."

Barbados Heroine

"Don't you stop over in Vegas?" Otis asked, while Alice took his drink order.

"Only for a few hours, then back to Miami and a few days off."

"Okay. I will see you when I return to Miami." Monica called her uncle.

"Good morning, uncle Otis," Monica said when he answered the phone.

"Who is this?" Otis asked.

"This is your niece Monica in England."

"Hello. How are you?"

"I am good. And you?"

"We are all good. How's your dad and the others?"

"They're all good," she continued. "Uncle. I'm going to Barbados on an extended stay, and I need a place to stay. I wanted to know if your house on the Island was available."

"When are you going? The house won't be available until next week after the guests have checked out."

"Next week? That's great. I'll book my flight."

"We may come down later in the year, not sure. I will let you know. Your aunt Evelyn will give you the keys when you get there."

"Thanks, uncle. I'll stay in touch."

"Take care, we'll talk again soon," Otis promised before hanging up the phone.

Sherwin A Goodman

Otis Williams, made his wealth investing in real-estate and in the import and export business. Otis didn't trust anyone outside of the two people he employed who has worked with him from the first day he opened Williams Import & Export, fifteen years later and the staff has increased by four, with the exception of his wife Alice.

Otis dealt in rare pieces of antique artifacts, sculptures, paintings and rugs.

His business dealing has caught the attention of individuals from the wrong side of the law as well as members of the law enforcement agency.

His wife Alice, an airline hostess for many years with American Airline, her seniority allowed her to choose when, and where she flies.

Alice and Otis were married in the Anglican church where Otis was a member.

Alice wore a white lace dress- made her a delightful bride. They honeymoon in Barbados where Alice got pregnant.

They had a baby boy..They named him Otis Dennis Williams Jr. That was thirty years ago. He now owns and operates two stripped clubs in the Miami area. Like his dad, Dennis loves the Las Vegas action, he's a better than average poker player and have won a couple of small Poker tournaments.

A play boy of sorts, juggling two women, Venessa Holiday in Miami, and Sarah Clarkson in Tampa Bay.

Barbados Heroine

"When are you going to settle down and give us some grand children?" his mother asked on his last visit to see them. That was a few weeks ago.

"I haven't thought about it," Dennis replied.

"Well, you should. None of us are getting any younger," Alice said.

"All in due time," Dennis said with a shrug and a raised brow.

The section that Otis uses for his office, was a spacious room with a big leather couch and a few matching chairs, a huge HD TV that took up one side of the office.

A large wall unit that also served as a mini bar stocked with his favorite alcohol beverage consists of single malt whiskey, also Hennessy Cognac, AKA the liquor of gods, and Grey Goose Vodka for his visiting associates.

There's an emergency door hidden behind the wall unit which Otis had install at the suggestion of his wife Alice when she found out about the two hooded gun men who had tried to rob his place of business a couple of years after it opened.

~ ~ ~

Monica made plans to open a hotel/casino business on the Island of Barbados. With her education in business administration and the knowledge of working at the London exchange, she's hoping it would be a success.

Through her and her dad's contacts, Monica put together a syndicate of interesting investors from the business sector of London to develop a multi-million dollar complex on the Island of Barbados.

Her mother Sybil had a going-away party for Monica, with only close friends and family members.

Soccer player Randolph Channing was a little over six feet tall, with curly black hair bleach on one side, and a physic body straight out of a male model catalog.

At twenty-eight, Randolph was one of the highest-paid football players in the English football league. Randy and Monica had been friends from childhood. He had a crush on her, but Monica would have no part of Randy in a romantic way. They remained friends after school.

Now, after her fiance Joseph's death, Randy was hoping Monica would reconsider and go out on a date with him.

Randy heard that Monica was going to Barbados to start a business there, and her mother was giving a going away party on her behalf.

Monica and Randy haven't seen each other for a long time. He was busy traveling with his football club, and she, with her work and grieving the lost of her fiance Joseph.

Barbados Heroine

Randy call Monica's parents residence.

"Hello. Who is this?" Sybil asked when she answered the phone.

"You forgot the sound of my voice? I am Randolph Channing," he raised a brow.

"Randy?" Sybil sighed. "How are you?"

"I'm good. How's everyone?"

"Randy. Why don't you come over this weekend? We're having a little get together for Monica, she's going to Barbados, and I am sure she'd love to see you before she leaves."

"I will be there," Randy promised before turning off his cell.

Randy arrived at the party at ten-thirty in the evening.

"It's been a long time, Randy. Welcome," Rosevelt said when he opened the door and saw Randy standing there.

"Yes. Too long," Randy replied when the two men shook hands.

"Come in!" Rosevelt commanded, stepping aside with a gesture.

Randy entered the house, and a few people were dancing to calypso music playing on the stereo.

Monica was in the kitchen and didn't hear when Randy came into the house.

"Where is Monica?" Randy asked Sybil when they greeted each other.

"She's in the kitchen," Sybil gestured with a

nod of her head in the kitchen's direction.

Randy followed the direction pointed out to him and found Monica with her back to the entrance opening a bottle of wine.

He tapped on the side of the kitchen. "Can I give you a hand with that?" he asked, raising a brow.

Monica looked around in astonishment and saw Randy with a smile on his face. She place the bottle of wine on the kitchen counter and took a step towards Randy.

They greeted each other with a hug and a kiss on the cheek.

"Hello, beautiful," he whispered in her ear.

"Hi, yourself," she replied.

"Still as beautiful as ever."

"Thank you. And you don't look a day older than when you left school."

"You're going away?"

"Yes. I leave for Barbados next Thursday."

"I understand you won't be back anytime soon?"

At that moment, her father entered the kitchen and took the wine out to the guest.

"Let's go out on the balcony," Monica suggested with a shrug.

Chapter 3

On the balcony, they sat down at the only table there. From the jacket pocket, Randy took a gift box.

"This was a going away gift for you." he delightfully said, looking into her face.

She took the box, opened it, and looked at the contents. "I can't take this, it's too much," Monica sighed, looking at the necklace along with matching earrings.

"I want you to have it. You still haven't told me when you're coming back."

"I won't be back for a while. I am starting a business in Barbados."

"What kind of business? You alone, or you

have partners?"

"Uncle Otis, my farther, and a few other investors my dad and I know."

"Can I get in on it? I have some cash lying around in the bank doing absolutely nothing. I might as well invest some of it with you."

"Are you sure?" Monica asked.

"Yes. I want in," Randolph said.

"It's going to cost you a substantial amount of money if you invest with us."

"You haven't told me about the business you're planning to open down there."

"It's a hotel/casino. There aren't any big gaming facilities on the Island, I've spoken to the people in the government who is responsible for such projects and got the green light and sign documents to go ahead."

"Through my uncle Otis contact on the Island. I got in touch with a surveyor named Jerry Kellman an Architect and a building contractor," Monica continued. "The surveyor found out that the owner of the land beside the property had erected a fence three feet too far inside our property."

"So. Work has already begun?" Randy asked curiously.

"Yes. The contractor has started work on the building."

"You haven't told me if I can get in on your project."

Barbados Heroine

"Of course you can."

"Okay, great."

"How much are you willing to invest?" Monica asked curiously.

"I'll leave that up to you."

"No. You have to make that decision yourself, " Monica suggested.

"Okay. Will you give me the information to take to my financial consultant at the bank?"

"Yes. You'll have it before you leave," Monica assured him.

They got up from the table and rejoined the other friends and family members in the house.

~ ~ ~

Monica arrived in Barbados on Thursday afternoon. Aunt Evelyn met her at the airport, and took her to Otis's house.

Friday morning, Monica call Sydney Crichlow.

"Good morning. Who's this?" Sydney asked.

"This is Monica Williams from London."

"Ah, yes. Miss Williams. Are you here on the Island?" Sydney raised a brow.

"Yes. I arrived yesterday afternoon."

"How long will you be staying?" Sydney asked curiously.

"I'll here indefinitely."

"When can you visit the building site?"

"Would tomorrow be alright?" she inquired. "I have other things to do today."

"Yes. I'll be there at ten o'clock in the morning, but many of the workmen will be on the site at seven o'clock," Sydney replied.

"Okay. I'll see you in the morning," Monica assured him.

"Oh. Have you spoken to Jerry Kellman?" Sydney Crichlow asked.

"Not yet. I will give Mr. Kellman a call later today," Monica shrugged.

"Until tomorrow then. Goodbye, Miss Williams," Sydney said before hanging up the phone.

The real estate owned by her parents was the perfect place for Monica to set up her business establishment. The property was located on the west side of the East coast road with a full view of the Atlantic Ocean.

Later on Friday afternoon, Monica called Jerry Kellman using her uncle Otis's house phone.

"Good afternoon Mr. Kellman," Monica said when Jerry answered the phone.

"Hello, Miss Williams. I have a copy of the land document from the surveyor that did the work on Mr. Gordon's property for you, and also a message from the owner," Jerry explained. "I can drop the papers off on my way home from the office."

Barbados Heroine

"That would be great, thank you," Monica continued. " I am looking forward to seeing you."

"Mr. Gordon, the man that owns the property would like to know if you'll take a cash payment for the piece of your land his fence was erected on by mistake?" Jerry Kellman inquired.

"Have you worked out how much of the property I would lose?"

"Yes, I have worked it out."

"Great."

"Why don't you come into my office a day next week and let's go over the situation before making your decision about the offer from Mr. Gordon?"

"How about Tuesday of next week?"Monica suggest.

"Great, let us say, 10.30 Tuesday morning!"Jerry Kellman said.

"Okay."

Jeremy Gordon had it all. A luxurious villa on the east coast of Barbados overlooking the Atlantic Ocean, where he stays six months a year. The other six months he spends in New York.

Jeremy has a mistress in New York and another one in Barbados.

After Jeremy Gordon's wife pass-away, he married the housekeeper, a woman from the Philippines named Alicia Ramos.

She was ten years younger than him when

Jeremy bought property in Barbados and build his dream house. She was all for it.

Jeremy wanted to be sure the contractor followed his specification for the building. His son would look after the business when Jerry was away.

On one of those return trips from Barbados. Jeremy noticed a long-distance phone number he didn't recognize. There were outgoing calls and collect calls from the same number on his phone bill.

Jeremy had already installed surveillance cameras outside of his home in New York. Unknown to his Philippino wife, Alicia Ramos, Jerry had the cameras installed and hidden in every room in the house.

Jeremy never questions his wife about the outgoing long-distance phone calls or the collect calls.

Tiny Saunders and Jeremy Gordon. The two men were buddies from school days. Tiny stood at 6 feet 8 inches tall and weighed 300 lbs.

Tiny went on and played football in the NFL. Jeremy. After getting a loan from a family member started his business. Jeremy never missed a home game. He was Tiny's number one fan.

When Tiny retired from playing football because of a busted knee, Jeremy offered him a job, the two men became inseparable.

Trips to Las Vegas and Atlantic city together,

they both enjoy the action and entertainment.

When Jeremy was building the house in Barbados, he would travel to the Island alone, leaving Tiny and his son to keep the business running smoothly.

Tiny never interrupted Alicia in her daily routine. He kept a detailed account of her movements in case Jeremy wanted to know what she did while he was in Barbados.

Jeremy returned from Barbados a few days earlier than scheduled. Tiny picked him up at the airport. "Is she at home?" Jeremy asked.

"No. Alicia went out earlier and hadn't returned," Tiny replied.

Arriving home, Jeremy and Tiny went to the basement and checked the video from inside the home.

The video clip shows Alicia, and a man enters the house through the door leading from the garage.

Both immediately undressed, leaving a trail of clothing leading to the bedroom.

"That bitch," Jeremy uttered.

"Alicia had the man laid in the back of the car so anyone won't see him," Tiny stated.

"Slut," Jeremy said, with the sound of anger in his voice.

"She's a piece of work," Tiny Injected. "After what you did for her, this is how she repays you."

"I've seen enough. Let's go upstairs and wait

for Alicia," Jerry suggests.

The two friends left the basement, went upstairs, and sat down at the bar.

"What are you going to do?" Tiny asked, as he headed behind the bar and took a bottle of Glenfiddich, and poured it into two glasses.

"Only one thing to do," Jeremy replied.

Minutes later, Alicia Ramos arrived home carrying two bags of store-bought items.

"Hi Darling, didn't know you were back," Alicia said as she kissed Jeremy on his cheek.

"Yes. I decide to come back early."

"Okay, I'll put these items away, then we can do something."

"I feel like watching a movie," Jeremy said.

"Great, if that's what you want."

"What are we going to watch?" Alicia asked went she rejoined Jeremy and Tiny at the bar.

Jeremy, Alicia, followed by Tiny, left the bar and went into the TV room. Tiny locked the door and put the key into his pocket. Jeremy placed the video into the machine and turned it on.

Alicia watched in disbelief as her image appeared on the screen.

The videotape had everything on it. She entering the house from the garage door followed by a man, kissing and undressing each other.

The bedroom scene came next. Alicia with her legs in the air and the man going down on her, she in-turned did the same to the man.

"Please stop the video, Jeremy. I'm so sorry," Alicia begged.

"Shut to fuck up, bitch. The only thing I want to hear from you. Who is the pipsqueak?"

"He's a nobody. Please stop it!

"What the fuck are you saying. A nobody doing things to you and making you beg for more?" Jeremy scream.

Alicia got up from her seat and tried to leave the room.

"Sit your ass back down and watch the fucking movie, bitch!" Jeremy commanded.

Alicia did as she was ordered too, seeing as how Tiny had also got up from his seat when she did.

Now Alicia began to shake with fear. She cringed in her seat, wondering what Jeremy will end up doing to her. She had heard stories at the hairdresser salon about Jeremy being a member of certain groups that nobody mess around with, not even the cops.

Chapter 4

Alicia sat and watch the rest of the video through half close eyes as the man got up from the bed and went into the bathroom. Moments later, both of them got dressed and went out the same way they had entered.

Tiny got up from his seat and turn the lights on, he then sat in the chair behind Alicia and rest his huge hand on her shoulder.

"This is the last time I'll ask you this question. Who is that man? I want his name and address?" Jeremy commanded, as Tiny handed her a piece of paper and a pen.

"Jeremy please. I'm so sorry," she'd pleaded, with tears running down her cheeks.

Barbados Heroine

"You'll be sorrier if you don't write his name and address on that piece of paper, you god damn fucking Asia whore."

Alicia wrote the name and address of the man on the piece of paper and handed it back to Tiny, who in-turn gave it to Jeremy.

"Angelo Cruz," Jeremy said out loud.

"What are you going to do?"

"You think I'll allow you to bring your fucking boyfriend into my home and fuck him without consequences. Then for you and him to have a good laugh about it, NEVER," Jeremy said nastily.

"He's not my boyfriend."

"He's not your boyfriend? You're telling me you just pick him up of the street, bring him into my house, and fucked him?"

"No. He's the father of my only child," Alicia explained.

"Child! What child?" Jeremy asked.

"My daughter."

"Fuck this. I heard enough," Jeremy said, and handed the note to Tiny. "Take care of this."

Tiny took the note and left the room, asking no questions.

Alicia Ramos and Angelo Cruz were never seen or heard from again.

Jeremy vowed never to get married again. The two buddies remained bachelors. That was a few years ago.

Marva Gittens/Haynes, the mistress in Barbados, also has a husband but somehow has time to keep Jeremy happy with their arrangement.

Marva Gittens, owns and operates two saloons where you can have your hair styles, also manicures and pedicures. Or you can make an appointment and have someone come to your home and perform the service.

One of the saloons situated in the city of Bridgetown, the other two situated in the Christ Church area in the shopping malls.

Marva's husband Larry Haynes,works on board a cruise ship traveling around the world which takes him away for many long voyages, and weeks at any given time.

The couple have no children, giving Marva plenty of free time to do what ever she feels like doing at any time she wishes in the absent of her husband.

Gabriel King, his New York mistress, operates her boutique with a staff of four other women, she was never married. Gabriel and Jeremy have been dating for over ten years.

When Jeremy and Gabriel first started dating, she got pregnant, he insisted and made her abort the baby which she did.

~ ~ ~

Each morning Monica worked out, using

various activities. Her stationary bike for one hour and a little weight lifting during the weekdays, and weekends, a jog, and walked around the park ground close to her home when she's in London.

Now she's in Barbados and thinking of ways to keep her exercise routine on track.

The sunlight filtered through the blinds in her bedroom windows and woke Monica.

It's Friday, and she has an appointment with the bank manager on transferring funds from her London bank into her Barbados bank account.

On Saturday, Monica arrived at the building site. The contractor Sydney Crichlow was there to meet her.

The contractor gave Monica a tour, and she became surprised at how fast the project was coming together.

"Do you have an estimated time for the completion of the hotel?" Monica asked Sydney.

"I'm looking at six more months, seven at the most."

"Can I advertise for the opening date of business six and a half months from now?"

"I don't see why not," Sydney continued. "There's no shortage of supplies, and I have many extra workers coming in on weekends to work on the building."

"That's great."

"I will let everyone know that hotel/casino is

on schedule for opening in late October," Monica said.

The building should be ready for the start of the tourist season that begins from November through March of the following year.

There will be two hundred and fifty rooms available for guests, a conference room capable of hosting one hundred and fifty people, a sports section with T V monitors bringing games from around the world, and a game room with slots machine and poker tables.

After the tour of the building site Saturday evening, on the drive back home, Monica stopped at her aunt Evelyn's house.

She picked up her portion of the Island Saturdays special meal comprise Black pudding and Souse with thin slices of Breadfruit, along with salt-fish cakes and turn-overs.

Sunday morning. Monica woke up at five O'clock and started her stretching exercises. Thirty minutes later, she walked five minutes to Miami Beach, a popular place for the residents and visitors.

People gather at that beach early in the mornings from five o'clock until ten.

Monica walked and enjoyed the sandy beach; birds were chirping in the nearby berry trees. Rooster crowing good morning in the distance, fishing boats were at anchor in the bay after delivering their cargo to the fish-market.

Barbados Heroine

The warm blue sea water runs for miles before going out to the open Caribbean ocean.

By midday, all the residents are out of the sea. They move away from the beach before the water becomes warm. Monica returned home at seven o'clock and made a breakfast of fruits with biscuits and tea.

At nine o'clock the house phone rang, and Monica picked up the receiver. "Hello, good morning," she said.

"Good morning, Cuz. Jennifer, here."

"Hey, Cousin Jennifer. How are you?"

"I'm good," Jennifer continued. " Mom told me to pick you up this morning on my way to church."

"Yes, she mentioned that to me yesterday. What time will you be here?"

"The service starts at eleven o'clock, and I'll pick you up at ten."

"Okay. I will be ready. See you later."

'Did you go to the beach?"Jennifer asked.

"Yes. Five-thirty this morning, I was in the water at Miami beach," Monica sighed with excitement.

"Good, that's the best time to go in the water, and be out before midday," Jennifer advised.

"Cool. I'll see you when you get here," Monica said before hanging up the phone.

Chapter 5

The family gathered at Evelyn's home after the church service for their Sunday cook-out. A feast of Rice and peas with pig-tails and sweet potato, baked macaroni with cheese pie, fried and baked chicken with salt-fish gravy and sweet coconut bread.

Monday, the two medium size container drums Monica had shipped to Barbados before leaving London arrived at the port. She had packed her exercise stationary bike along with her computer and food items into the two drums.

After paying the duty on the two drums, Monica hired a delivery van to bring them to her residence. The remainder of the day, Monica unpacked the items from the containers, then put away the food items, reassembles her work out bicycle, and set up the computer.

Tuesday morning, Monica arrived at the surveyor's office for her appointment with Mr. Jerry Kellman.

"Good morning, Miss Williams," Jerry said, opening his office door.

"Good morning Mr. Kellman."

"Come in and take a seat!" he offered, stepping back to allow Monica to enter the office.

She sat down on one chair facing Mr. Kellman.

"Did you have any problem finding the building?"

"No. It wasn't hard," Monica shrugged.

"Did you look at the neighbor's fence on your property when you visited the building on Saturday?"

"Yes, I did."

"Have you decided what you will do about the fence?" Jerry raised a brow.

"No. I wanted to talk with you to get your input before talking to my parents about it."

"It's thirty feet of land you will lose if you decide to accept his offer."

"That means, getting a lawyer to file new documents with the court about the deed for the property," Monica sighed.

"Yes. You'll have to do that," Jerry advised.

"How could the surveyor he hired made such a mistake? Why didn't the surveyor search for the old markers before putting down new one?"

"The excuse was, he couldn't find any of the original land markers,"Jerry Kellman said.

"That's rubbish."

"Mr. Gordon and I didn't have a lengthy conversation about the fence."

"I don't want him to think I'm un-neighborly, but his fence is on my property," Monica said furiously.

"I know sometimes these things happened, either by mistake or deliberately. I'm not sure about this one," Jerry raised a brow.

"Any advice from you about what you think is best for me."

"My advice is to talk to your parents before making your decision or talking to the lawyer," Jerry continued. "You should take into account the cost to file the deed and how much the lawyer will charge you for the service."

"I will talk with Mr. Gordon and find out if he's prepared to pay for everything. The price of the property, lawyer fees, and court cost before calling my parents," Monica said.

"This is the phone number where you can reach him," Jerry Kellman said, handing a card with a number written on it to Monica.

"May I use your phone? I will try to reach him

now."

"Sure you can," Jerry said.

Monica dialed the number on the card and waited for an answer.

"Hello," the voice of a woman said.

"I am Monica Williams from London. May I speak with Mr. Gordon?"

"Hold on, please!" the woman replied.

Moments later. "Hello Miss Williams, I'm Jeremy Gordon."

"I Receive your request from Mr. Kellman," Monica said.

"Yes. I ask Mr. Kellman to have you contact me about the fence," Gordon said.

"I would like to know if you're willing to cover the cost of having this problem fix. Court and lawyer fees and the money for the property?"

"Of course. I will."

"Can I get back to you in a few days with my decision?"

"I will be here for another few weeks before going to New York."

"Okay. I will be in touch before you leave," Monica promised.

"All right. Until I hear from you, goodbye for now."

"Goodbye," replied Monica before hanging up the phone.

"I will wait to hear from you before filing the papers on the property," Jerry informed Monica.

"Good bye, Mr. Kellman. I'll be in touch," Monica assured Jerry while getting up from the chair.

"Goodbye. Miss Williams," Jerry said while opening his office door for Monica to leave.

Stephany Williams, sister of Monica and Co-founder of the magazine Blacks In Action "B I A" with her best friend Lolita Greaves from their days attending school together..

Stephany, a wise woman at such a young age. She'd observed much in her young life, both good and bad.

Stephany Williams followed in her big sister footsteps and studied literature at the University of London. After graduating, she started training as an assistant editor, having experience in journalism writing the monthly school paper.

Young, smart, and very beautiful; it wasn't long before the guys at the office began hitting on her.

One such guy was Oliver Compton, a tall, handsome, and dangerous-looking young man with broad shoulders.

He was white, which she knew would not please her parents, should she choose to go out with Oliver.

Still, Stephany kept hoping that Oliver would ask her for a date. He was the only one of the young men she fancied.

Without her knowledge. Oliver had gathered

information from one of her school friends about her likes and dislikes. Then one Friday afternoon, he stopped by her desk.

"I have two tickets to the Beyonce concert this coming weekend at Hyde Park. Would you like to attend it with me?" Oliver asked Stephany with an enormous smile.

"Yes. Of course. I will go with you," Stephany happily answered with a glamorous and surprise look on her face.

"Shall I pick you up?" Oliver asked.

"No. Let's meet someplace near to the concert and go from there," Stephany suggested.

"Okay. We'll meet at Park Park lane, and then go to Hyde Park," Olive said.

Stephany and Oliver had a ball and enjoyed their first date together at the concert.

"Will you go out with me again?" Jerry asked after the concert was over.

"I'll think about it."

"Fair enough."

Stephany and Oliver walked from Hyde Park back to where their cars were parked. They hugged each other in a friendly way and said goodnight.

Lolita Greaves was the daughter of James Greaves and Cindy Stuart/Greaves.

After her graduation from college where she had took drama classes, Lolita tried to get into the film industry, that's where she meet a young up and coming actor named Larry Somers.

The two dated for a couple of month until they attended a birthday party given in the honor of a film director.

Lolita got angry with Larry after he began flirting with another young lady.

"You shouldn't walk around with a pissed-off expression!" Larry said to Lolita.

"I'm so angry with you," Lolita replied. "Why did you leave me standing here and go talking and touching that other girl?"

"It's nothing."

"Nothing? Lolita said, her brown eyes flashing major signs of danger.

"You know how it is in this business, you have to be friendly with everyone."

"First I saw you talking and laughing with the guy who is serving the drinks, and the next thing I know, you're doing the same with that girl."

"Her name is Jean Mitchell, and she was in the last movie I appeared in, she's nice and a good friend."

"Really," Lolita said. "It looked more than just friends to me. What did she play, your lover?"

"She played as a receptionist," Larry said trying to calm Lolita down.

"Is she fucking the director to get the invite to this function, or you?"

"You're behaving very bitchy,"Larry said, baiting her.

"Me, bitchy? I'm just mentioning what I saw."

Barbados Heroine

"You wouldn't be jealous, would you?" Larry said, with a grin.

"Of course not," Lolita replied. "But, a little more attention to your date, which I am would be nice."

"You have to mix, interact with other guest, you never know who you might bump into, might be a director or producer looking for someone like you."

"I know, but I don't want to come across as free and available," Lolita said.

"Believe me, no one will notice, these party are classy, not some pick-up social gathering," Larry informed her.

Then the unexpected happened, the girl he said was in his last movie came over, took Larry by the hand and led him away from Lolita.

Larry didn't protest against the interruption of the conversation he was having with Lolita.

She liked Larry, he always acted like a gentleman opening and closing the car door for her each time she got in and out of the vehicle.

Now on their second date, and Larry has not tried to give her a romantic kiss, only a smooch on the cheek at the end of their dates.

Monday morning, after the weekend party, Lolita's cell phone rang. "Hello," Lolita said when she answered.

"This is the extras casting agent, I have a part for you in a movie being shot at the moment if you're interested."

"Of course I am."

"I'll send you the information, you have to be on time."

"I'll be on time," Lolita assured the agent.

Lolita worked for the last three days of the shoot making a bit of much needed cash. Larry was also a member of the movie cast. He got his first speaking role in this film.

"Will you go with me this weekend to the celebration of completing the filming of the movie?" Larry asked Lolita when they walked from the movie set heading for the parking lot.

"Sure," Lolita replied.

"Kool, I'll pick you up around ten pm."

"Okay, see you tomorrow," Lolita said.

The party was a casual affair for the cast and crew.

Larry and Lolita arrived at the party around ten-thirty pm. The room was filled with the aroma of expensive cigars and cologne.

"Hi Larry, hi Lolita,"Jean Mitchell said when she walked up to greet them.

"Hi, when did you get here?" Larry asked.

"A little while ago," Jean replied. "William was asking for you."

"Okay, I'll find him,"Larry said, then walked away leaving Lolita and Jean.

"Who is William?" Lolita asked Jean.

"It's best you asks Larry, I won't want to give

you the wrong impression about William."

"Okay, I need a drink," Lolita said.

"The bar is at the back," Jean explained while pointing to the back of the room.

"I'll find it,"Lolita said as she walked away from Jean.

While heading to the bar, Lolita saw the silhouette of two people in a tent that was erected on the back lawn embracing, then one of them tenderly touch the other's cheek. Lolita got a bit of a shock when she saw the two people emerged, it was none other than Larry and another man.

Lolita thought to herself.

That's the reason he never kissed her after the dates or tried to make love, he's gay, a man lover.

Moments later, Lolita left the party and never went on another date with Larry.

Lolita continued working as an extra in the movies hoping one day to be discovered, but the opportunity never came.

Chapter 6

Weeks after that party fiasco, Lolita ran into her old school mate Stephany and they had lunch together.

"What you been up too?" Stephany asked.

"Doing work as an extra in the movies," replied Lolita.

"Meet any famous actors?" Stephany asked.

"I never got the chance to be close to any of them."

"What are you working on now?"

"Nothing at the moment. What about you? What are you up too these days?"

"I'm thinking about starting my own business."

"What kind of business are you planning to

start?"

"A magazine, I have this idea about black business owners that many people of color don't know about. This could give them the exposure they're missing."

"Sounds like a good idea, you need a partner?"

"Hell yes. You and me, man we'll make this work," Stephany excitingly replied.

"I'm kinda short on funds, I'll hit up my dad for a loan," Lolita shrugged.

That's the day they came up with the idea of doing something together, and the magazine B.I.A "Blacks In Action" was created.

~ ~ ~

Theodore Williams met this woman named Jasmine Howell on the internet. He told her he was thirty-six years of age when, in fact, he was only twenty-two. Jasmine was forty years old and a divorced woman with one child aged eleven.

Theodore had set up his profile as a man with an interest in women of any age. He had recently lost his childhood sweetheart a beautiful redhead name Hannah Storm, and he was very lonely.

Theodore and Hannah dated all through their high school days, then shortly after graduating, Hannah's dad took a overseas Diplomatic post with the British government taking the family with him.

Sherwin A Goodman

The two young lovers stayed in touch for awhile then the long distance love affair fell apart

Theodore and his buddy Alex shared an apartment and began to frequent the night clubs and engaged with women having many one night affairs.

One night while out prowling the night clubs, they hooked up with a couple of bombshells cousins, named Mavis Moore and Millie Moore better known as M and M.

"I'm going to the Loo, order me a beer will you," Theodore said to Alex when they entered the night club.

"Okay."

At the bar, Alex notice the two girls sitting on stools at the end of the bar and move closer to them.

"Hi, ladies," Alex said leaning against the bar to order the drinks.

"Hi, yourself," one of the girls replied.

"I'm Millie and this is my cousin Mavis," the other girls stated.

"I'm Alex and my friend Theodore went to the Loo."

"Is he handsome like you?" Mavis asked.

"You'll see for yourself when he gets here."

When Theodore returned from the Loo and joined Alex, Mavis left her seat.

"You are more handsome than your friend," Mavis said when she stood touching Theodore.

Barbados Heroine

"Thank you, and you're very beautiful," Theodore replied.

"Let's dance!" Mavis held his hand and headed for the dance floor leaving Alex and Millie chatting.

The four of them left the night-club together and went to Theodore and Alex's apartment.

Theodore open a couple of bottles of wine, then put on a sex movie on the TV, then had a night of four-some. Soon after, Alex got his own apartment and moved out, but the duo continued to pick up girls when they go out clubbing.

That was before Theodore met Jasmine online.

Jasmine was recently divorced and also a member of the lonely hearts club.

Jasmine and her husband Richard Howell were married for twelve years. Richard was a stay at home dad, taking care of the couple's young son after losing his job when the company he worked for relocated from London to Dublin.

Taking their son school, Richard came in contact with many other parents at the school, mostly women.

Elizabeth Sheppard, a curvy blonde woman, Richard couldn't resist her flirting and decided to take her up on her flirts.

One day after dropping of their children at school, they went back to Elizabeth flat.

As fate would have it, Jasmine was in the area showing a house to prospective buyers, after the showing while driving along the street she noticed Richard's car parked on the street, knowing there's no reason for him to be there, Jasmine parked her car and waited to see which house he was visiting.

A few minutes after Jasmine parked her vehicle, she saw Richard stepped out of a door and stopped then a blonde hair female hugged and kissed him then close the door while Richard got into his car and drove away. A few months later they were divorced.

~ ~ ~

And seeing this handsome young black man's profile, she flirted with him on the internet. But then Theodore's persistence got the better of her, and they made plans to meet.

Theodore booked a table for two at Harry's restaurant to have dinner with Jasmine. He also requested the table to be round.

Theodore and his best friend, Alex Smith, who's also twenty-two years of age, were inseparable buddies. Alex, like Theodore, had also set-up a phony profile on the internet about liking older women, and when Jasmine agreed to meet with Theodore, Alex felt like he was also having the date with her.

Later on, the afternoon of the day that Jasmine and Theodore were to hookup for their date, Alex came over to Theodore's house to chill.

Barbados Heroine

"I want to meet your internet woman," Alex instructed, sipping on a bottled beer.

"You'll meet her. My car is still in the shop; you have to give me a ride to the restaurant."

Alex was six feet one inch with a muscular body and dreadlocks, thick lips, long arms, and wears a size thirteen shoes.

Like Theodore, Alex's parents emigrated to London from the Island of Barbados.

His dad was a prominent lawyer, and his mother became a registered nurse. Theodore and Alex worked at the Samsung office in Battersea. The two young men were friends from school days, going to the same school and graduating the same year.

Theodore was the first of the two to get at Samsung, Alex joined the company six months later.

Theodore got dressed, then got into Alex's car, and they headed for Harry's restaurant. Arriving at the restaurant, Theodore and Alex entered and was ushered to the table Theodore had reserved.

The waiter gave them a cocktail menu and a dinner menu.

"Care to have something from the bar before ordering your meal?" the waiter asked.

"I'm expecting a lady to join me for dinner," Theodore explained. "Her name's Jasmine, will you show her to my table when she arrive."

"I'm his driver for tonight," Alex injected

before the waiter asks any more questions.

Minutes later, Jasmine arrived at the restaurant. Theodore got up from his seat when the waiter brought her to the table.

"Hello, Jasmine," Theodore said with an outstretched hand.

Jasmine took his hand. "Hello, Theodore. It's nice to finally meet you."

"This is my friend and driver for tonight, Alex," Theodore gesturing to his friend.

"Hi. Alex," Jasmine responded with a nod.

"Hello," Alex replied. "I'll leave you two to enjoy your dinner."

"Okay, Alex. I'll call you when I am ready for a ride back home."

"No need to do that," Jasmine said. "I can give you a ride back to your home."

Theodore got up from his seat and walked with Alex to the exit of the restaurant.

Jasmine found that she couldn't stop staring at the two young men while they walked away from the table.

Suddenly, Theodore glanced around and met her stare. Their eyes met, but he didn't look away, and neither did she.

At that moment, she thought. Was this going to be the man she will have an affair with.

Jasmine experienced a little excitement, then a pulse feeling between her legs while she sat and wait for Theodore to return to the table.

Barbados Heroine

It had been a long time since a man romantically touched her. She was full of desire for Theodore.

What am I going to do? She thought. I must be crazy, lusting after this young man whom I just met. But her heart was telling her to go for it.

On the way back to the table, Theodore stopped by the bar and ordered a Bohemian cocktail for Jasmine, and a Chivas regal for himself.

The waiter brought the drinks to the table and took their dinner order.

Looking at the menu, Jasmine couldn't decide what to have.

"I'll order for both of us," Theodore suggested.

"Splendid Idea," Jasmine replied.

He then ordered a salad for both of them, and for the main course, he chooses the Chateaubriand steak for two with truffle and Madeira sauce, and from the wine section, Theodore ordered a bottle of Cabernet Sauvignon.

The restaurant was impeccable with a lively atmosphere.

One hour later, Theodore paid the dinner bill.

"Shall we go?" He asked Jasmine.

"Yes, lets."

He then went around the table and pulled back the chair for Jasmine to stand. Theodore held her by the elbow when they went out the door.

Once outside, Jasmine tucked her hand under

Theodore's fore-arm, while they walked through the parking lot to her car.

"Why don't you drive," suggested Jasmine standing close to Theodore while handing him the keys to her car.

He moved in for a kiss, which she accepted with no objection. The sweetness of his thick lips made her body tingle. And that feeling of pulsing between her legs, with a weakness in her feet.

While he sucked on her soft lips for a moment before French kissing her.

Theodore opened the passenger side door and waited for Jasmine to get in before closing the door of the Audi.

He got behind the wheel and drove out of the parking area, then headed for his apartment.

Arriving at the building. "Do you want to come up for a coffee or something?" Theodore asked, still sitting behind the wheel of the Audi.

"Yes, I will. But I won't stay long. It's a thirty minutes drive to my home." Jasmine agreed, knowing she needed more than coffee to satisfy the pulsing between her legs.

Chapter 7

"I understand. You can leave whenever you're ready," Theodore said while switching off the car engine. He then got out, went around to the passenger door, and opened it for Jasmine.

She clenched his arm while they walked to his apartment.

Once inside, Jasmine sat on the sofa in the living room and took off her shoes while Theodore went to the kitchen and turned on the coffee making machine.

He left the kitchen and went back to the living room to join Jasmine; she stood up from the couch when Theodore got close and went into his arms, kissing him on his lips while her hand caress his body.

Theodore was caught off guard but quickly reacted as his two powerful hands cupped her ass bringing even closer to him.

Jasmine began to unbutton his shirt, as Theodore unzipped the back of her dress. She then unbuckle the belt from his trousers letting fall to the floor.

Jasmine took Theodore's fingers and began looking at them before playfully sucking them. He moaned with delight while she licked and sucked his cock. Theodore reached down and pulled Jasmine to her feet, then took off her clothes slowly.

Her two lovely breasts fell out of the bra, and he sucked them one at a time.

She whispered in his ear. "I love the way your tongue circled my nipples. I'm so turned on,take me now," Jasmine commanded.

She lay down on the sofa while he spread her legs and began kissing her navel, making a trail down her body.

"I love the way you taste," he whispered.

"Take me! I want to feel you in me, all of you."

Theodore enter her, while the sound of pleasure escaped her lips at the feel of him filling her.

"You feel so big and sweet, give me all of it," she whispered in his ear, running her tongue over his cheek.

"Yes. I will, and I will make love to you all night."

"I'm all yours, do whatever you want. Don't stop!"

~ ~ ~

Monica called her parents in London, England. Her father answered the phone.

"Hi, dad. How's everyone doing?"

"We're good. What about you and your project?"

"It's on schedule. I'm hoping to be open for business in six months."

"I sent an envelope down to you by registered mail containing essential papers, power of attorney, and ownership along with other documents in case you should need them."

"All right. I wanted to talk to you about the situation with the person who bought the property next to ours; his name is Jeremy Gordon."

"What happened?"

"Mr. Gordon has erected a fence three feet wide by ten feet long onto our property," Monica continued. "I need you to advise me on what I should do."

"What excuse did he give for erecting the fence that far on our land?"

"He said that he was in New York when the work was done. His girl-friend had hired someone she knew to erect the fence, and he didn't know it was over on our property until he was notified by us."

"Now that he knows, is he going to take it down?"

"He needs to know if I would accept cash for the piece of land? He's willing to pay for the cost of the property and the lawyer and court fees with the filing of documents," Monica explained to her father.

"Losing that much land. Is it going to affect the building?"

"I asked the contractor, and his reply was no. It wouldn't."

"I'll leave it up to you. I trust your judgment."

"Okay, dad. Is my mother at home? Oh, here is my new cell phone number I changed it to a local number here in Barbados."

"Wait, let me write it down. And, yes. Hold on, let me get your mother!"

"Hi, daughter, how's it going?" Sybil asked after taking the phone from her husband.

"I'm doing okay. What about you?" Monica asked sweetly.

"I'm good, the family is excellent. Will you be coming back home before the opening of the hotel?"

"Yes, I will. But I'm not sure of the date. I will keep you guys up to date."

"All right, take care," her mother sighed.

Barbados Heroine

"You too and give my love to Theodore and Stephany."

"I will. They are both out and about," Sybil shrugged quietly before hanging up the phone.

Being bored is a state of mind for some people, and today Jeremy Gordon found himself in that state of mind. He craved action regularly, and after his Barbadian mistress was on a cruise somewhere with her husband, he did not feel like sitting around the house alone.

And now after the long meeting with Monica and her lawyer,

Jeremy needed a little excitement. He was in the mood for something new, a sexy young girl to stay with him for the weekend. She had to be a knockout and willing, but not a prostitute in case Jeremy wanted to take her out, and she had to be fair-skinned.

His gardener Tony was the person Jeremy goes too whenever he needed someone younger than his mistress for a one-night stand.

"I need a young and sexy young girl for the weekend," Jeremy informed Tony. "With all the requirements. Is that going to be a problem?"

"I'll make a few calls. What day do you want her here?"

"Friday. That gives you one day."

Tony had done this for Jeremy before, but only for a one-night stand. Now, it's for the weekend that starts in one day.

Sherwin A Goodman

Tony made a few calls to his contacts and was given the phone number of a young lady who fitted the description of the woman he was looking for. He dial the number and arrange to meet with her before inviting her to meet with Jeremy.

The girl Tony had set Jeremy up with was from Brazilian, her dad was a Barbadian who had lived in Brazil for ten years, and dated her mother for awhile then moved back to Barbados not knowing he had made her mom pregnant.

~ ~ ~

She was twenty-three, five feet ten inches tall, and a knockout. Her name was Francisca, and Tony assured Jeremy that she wasn't a prostitute.

Francisca was dressed in a floral skirt and a low-cut blouse that showed the fullness of her breasts, which Jeremy couldn't keep his eyes off and a pair of Vionic Kirra sandals on her feet.

"Where did you find this one? Not that I don't trust you," he asked Tony after the introduction.

"She works at the Beach Club five days a week and has the weekend off."

"She's off from work every weekend?" Jeremy asked softly with excitement in his voice.

"What are you thinking?"

"I was planning to leave for New York because of Marva and her husband cruise. If Francisca turns out to be half as good of what I've heard about Brazilian women, then I'll stay and have her visit every weekend."

"I'll be on my way. I'll leave that arrangement between the two of you."

"Have a great weekend. I'll see you Monday," Jeremy promised.

"Yes. See you Monday, have a great weekend."

"I intend too."

Jeremy then turned to Francisca. "Care for a drink?" he asked.

"Baileys, if you have," she answered in the best Bajan dialect she could muster.

"Baileys, coming right up. And make yourself comfortable."

Francisca didn't wait to be told a second time to get comfortable. She took off the blouse and sandals, then sat down on the couch when Jeremy handed her the glass of Baileys.

He sat down beside her on the sofa. Surprise took Jeremy when Francisca reached over and played with the back of his neck. The feel of her soft hand was so soothing that Jeremy moved closer and put his head on the left side of her stomach.

"Tell me a little about yourself," he said.

"I moved here to live with my father six months ago, after my mother passed away."

"Your dad. What does he do?"

"He works on the ships. He's a sailor," Francisca shrugged.

"Tony tells me you're free from your job on weekends."

"Yes, I am off on weekends. Why?"

"Oh, nothing," Jeremy replied, not wanting to make any commitment before getting to know her a little before, and he has three days to do it.

The car sputtered and then came to a halt. Alex got out, popped the hood open, and inspected the engine. He checked the oil, antifreeze, and power steering fluids. Seeing nothing wrong, he then called his best friend Theodore.

"What's up, Alex?" Theodore asked.

"My car just died on me."

"Where are you?"

"I'm on Falcon Rd in Clapham Junction. I was on my way back from Gatwick airport."

"I'll come and get you."

~ ~ ~

Damn! This was not the way Alex had planned the evening. After finally getting a date with Lauren Alleyne, a girl he wanted to go out with for quite some time.

~ ~ ~

He had made a dinner reservation for Friday night and purchase tickets to the Rihanna concert for Saturday. Now, after this unexpected setback,

Barbados Heroine

Alex was becoming more and more frustrated with the broken-down car.

If his friend Theodore would be busy with his new woman this weekend and need his car, then he would have to rent a vehicle for a few days. "Alex thought to himself." While waiting for Theodore to arrive.

He had planned after returning from the airport. Alex would take a shower, then leave home around seven-thirty, go and pick Lauren up for their dinner date, and see where it goes from there.

A few moments later, his friend arrived.

"Have you called for a tow truck?" Theodore asked after parking his car ahead of Alex's broken down vehicle.

"No. I decided to wait and let us check the engine together."

"Okay. Let's have a look!" Theodore exclaimed with a gesture of his hand.

"I'll try to start the engine while you look under the hood."

Theodore walked around to the side of the car and watch, while Alex tried to start the vehicle.

"Stop!" Theodore yelled and beckoned Alex to join him.

"What is it?"

"You broke the fan belt," Theodore said while pointing at the damaged piece of mechanism.

"I didn't look at it; I checked the fluids, gas,

oils, and coolant but didn't look at the fan-belt."

"You need a tow truck to take it to a garage for repairs," Theodore suggested.

"I must get a rental car for the weekend. I have a hot date with Lauren, which I intend to keep."

"Nonsense about renting a vehicle. You can use mine. Jasmine will be coming over. It's the weekend that her son stays with his father, and in case we need to go out, we'll use her car."

Alex called the tow truck and waited with Theodore for the arrival.

"Jasmine seemed to be serious about the two of you."

"I'm thinking the same thing."

"She works?" Alex asked.

"Yes. Self-Employed. Jasmine has a real estate company, and she employs five other people."

The tow truck arrived and took the car to Alex's mechanic garage to have the repairs done. The vehicle was left in the parking lot because the garage was closed to business for the weekend, as pre-arranged with his mechanic Alex had permission to leave his car if anything should happen when the shop was closed.

Chapter 8

It's the weekend. Saturday morning, Monica was awakened by an early morning phone call from her sister Stephany. The call came through on her cell.

"What's up, sis?" Monica asked, struggling to wake up.

"Did I wake you?" Stephany asked.

"Yes. You forgot we're five hours behind here in Barbados."

"Oh dear. I am sorry," Stephany sighed.

"How you doing? I didn't get the chance to

talk with you the last time I called home."

"Yeah. Mom and dad mentioned that you'd call."

"I'm thinking about running an ad for the opening date of the hotel and would like you to do it in your magazine "B I A."

"No problem. We can run the ad in the magazine. Let me know when the hotel would be ready for business, and the date you'll like the ad to start."

"As of now, it's on schedule to be ready for opening in October."

"That's great. The magazine runs bi-weekly, we can start the ad in July."

"Good. I have to arrange the entertainment for the opening, and also plan the menu," Monica shrugged.

"What about the staff? Have you begun to interview prospective employees?"

"Not yet. I'm planning to have a sign erected on the site next week with the contact information for the hiring of staff."

"You have a place to carry out the interviews?"

"No. Will shop around for a small office space to conduct the interviews. I'll start with the email system for now until I have a place set up."

"What about help? You'll need someone to help you with the replies to the emails," Stephany suggested.

"I know. Cousin Jennifer will help me on the weekends. She's off on Saturday and Sunday from her regular job."

"Okay, sis. I'll let you go back to bed."

"Gee, thanks. I'm up now. I will exercise for a few minutes, then go to the beach for a swim in the sea."

"I would like a sea bath at this very moment. Take care, love you," Stephany said sweetly before hanging up her phone.

After returning home from her sea bath, Monica tried calling Sydney Critchlow, the building contractor. She got his answering machine and left a message for him to call her back at his earliest convenience.

Jennifer, every couple of weeks, she would take a trip to Trinidad and visit her lover, who's married to another woman.

She liked to party, after a fail marriage at a young age, and then a couple of disastrous affairs. Jennifer would find a party to attend, either in Barbados or Trinidad.

After the way her last relationship ended, which nearly costs Jennifer her life at the hands of the man she was dating.

He went into a jealous rage when Jennifer went on a boat cruise with members of her family, and he suspected that she'd gone with another man.

Ever since, the last boyfriend attacked and beat her vigorously, leaving her for dead. Jennifer had somehow managed to dial 911 for help, which saved her life.

On Friday, she received a text from her lover in Trinidad informing her not to visit on the weekend.

The humidity was high for the last few days. Saturday afternoon Jennifer called Monica.

"Hi cousin Jennifer," Monica said, answering her cell.

"I'm coming to your place, and I have your Saturday pudding and souse with slice breadfruit that my mother prepared," Jennifer explained.

"What time will you be here?"

"I'll be there in an hour. Were you planning to go out?"

"I was thinking of going to the pharmacy to get something. I have a slight headache."

"I'll get something for your headache."

One hour later, Jennifer pulled her car into the driveway at the front of uncle Otis's house, where Monica was staying.

"Come in, Jenn!" Monica exclaimed while opening the door.

"This is for you," Jennifer said, handing the sack containing the food and the pain medication to Monica.

"Thanks. How much I owe you for the pills?"

"Ah, don't worry about it. How's the head? Still hurting?"

"Not like earlier, don't know what brought that

on."

"I can think of one or two things," Jennifer said sweetly.

"What are they?"

"Do you think it's the humidity? It's high these last couple of days, and your body is still adjusting."

"You could be right."

"If not. When was the last time you got fucked?"

"A long time ago, when my boyfriend was still alive."

"I'm going to a party tonight given by my B F F Roxanne, and I would like you to go with me. She's an M P in the present government, many sitting politicians and local celebrities will be there."

"If I'm feeling better when you're ready to go," I'll love to attend."

"You could get lucky. Roxanne parties always have many attractive and single men in attendance," Jennifer raised a brow.

"I have plenty on my plate at the moments to get involved with a man," Monica said with a shrug

"You don't think about sex at all?"

"It's a healthy thing to think about sex. There's nothing wrong with that. Getting involved with a man just for sex is not healthy," Monica sighed.

"If you decide to come with me, I'll pick you

up at eleven tonight. I hope you can make it because they will be people in attendance that you should meet who can give you advice on the opening of your hotel," Jennifer explained.

"Yes. I'll go with you."

"I took the scenic route along the east coast road on my way here; the building is already two floors up, many vehicles were parked on the street, I couldn't find a place to park my car," Jennifer shrugged.

"The contractor mentioned that he has many workers that come and work with him on Saturdays and Sundays from their regular weekday jobs," Monica explained.

"I will leave now and let you take something for your headache," Jennifer said, heading for the door.

"I went to bed late last night, then my sister Stephany called and woke me up early this morning. She forgot that they're five hours ahead of us here in Barbados," Monica shrugged slightly.

"Maybe what you need is rest," Jennifer looked back at her and suggested with a sigh.

After spending time with Monica and assuring her she'll feel better after getting some rest. Jennifer got into her car while the rain began to fall. Before driving off, she made a call through whatsapp to her lover in Trinidad.

"Is something wrong?" he asked after answering the call somewhat harshly.

Barbados Heroine

"You don't seem too pleased to hear from me," Jennifer questioned Victor, feeling a little disappointed by the tone of his voice.

"I wasn't expecting to hear from you today, that's all."

"Where are you at the moment?"

"I'm at home."

"I would like you to explain to me the reason you don't need me to visit you this weekend. I was looking forward to it and you have disappointed me very much.

"Something came up.

"Something like what? Why can't you say what's going on?"

Victor Hernandez thought for a while before answering Jennifer's question."The wife had planned with members of her family for this weekend together, and I didn't know about it until Friday, then I text you the moment I heard about it."

"Why are you still at home? You're not going with them?" "I had a few things to do at the office. I'll drive out there in an hour or two." "When will I see you again?" Jennifer asked. "Or better still. Come to Barbados next weekend." "Yeah, brilliant idea. I'll see how the week goes, but I'm not making any promises, you understand." "Yes. I understand." "Okay, I'll let you know."

"All right, I'll wait to hear from you before making any plans," Jennifer promise before turning off the phone and driving away from the house.

Monica felt fortunate to have such a great family, members in the USA, in Barbados and the UK. Monica always felt she would become a savvy businesswoman with all the right instincts. The first time Monica made plans for starting a business with her fiance, Joseph Gibbs came to a halt when he was stabbed to death while crossing the Westminster Bridge in London, England. It's six pm, after lying in bed for a few hours. Monica woke up feeling much better.

She accepted her cousin Jennifer's invitation and attend the party with her later in the night. Monica dialed Jennifer's number.

"Hello, Monica. Are you feeling better?" Jennifer asked after answering her cell phone.

"Yes, I am. I will go out with you tonight."

"Kool. I'll pick you up around eleven o'clock tonight."

"I'll be ready," Monica assured her before hanging up the phone.

Monica stood before the mirror examining her hair. It satisfied her with the way it looked. Monica had visited the hair salon a couple of days earlier and had her hair touched up by the stylist. Tonight Monica wore a navy blue asymmetric hem one-shoulder dress with white Remix sandals, matching earrings and purse, with a pearl-studded bracelet.

Barbados Heroine

Jennifer picked up Monica at eleven o'clock and ventured of to the party. Arriving, they were greeted by the host MP Mariam Spencer, with a hug and a smile.

"I have heard many things about you," Mariam said to Monica.

"Hope what you've been told were all good," Monica replied.

"I heard it from Jennifer." "Yes, Jennifer told me you're a beautiful and friendly person to have as a friend." "Jennifer and I go a long way back, from school days and we stay close after leaving school."

Jennifer left Monica and Mariam chatting and mingled with the crowd.

"How's your project coming along?" Mariam asked and continued. "Have you set an opening date?" "At the moment, it's ahead of schedule. I'm hoping to open the establishment in early September."

"Why don't we have lunch next week and discuss this in more detail!" "I'll like that," Monica agreed. "You must excuse me. I see other guests are arriving." "Okay," Monica said while moving to mingle with the other guest.

She walked into the room and thought it looked fantastic. The tables were set with green and yellow cloths, the brass candlesticks,flatware, and crystal shine.

The plates were rimmed with silver it was

obvious that Mariam had put a lot of thought into tonight's event. The tables were set apart from the space provided for the dancing area.

Jennifer was on the dance floor with a man dancing to Calypso music. While Monica went to the bar and ordered a Cognac.

"Cuz, this is Mark Mayers, an old flame of mine," Jennifer said while introducing Mark to Monica. They shook hands and Mark walked away to join two guys that were standing in a corner of the room.

"An old flame?" Monica quizzed, raising a brow after Mark walked away

"Yes."

"Let me guess, he's also married."

"Of course he was. Now he's saying that they've split up."

"Do you believe him?"

"Not sure if I do."

"And you're aiming to find out? Aren't you?"'

"I'm thinking about it."

"Well. Don't let me stop you."

"Come on, let's dance! It's a party, so let's party. Show me some of those UK dance moves!"

Two hours later, Monica was ready to leave the party.

During the time spent at the event, she received many cards from some attending guests, which she took. Monica planned to sit down with Jennifer and go over the cards before getting in touch with anyone.

After taking Monica home from the party, Jennifer returned to the event and hook-up with Mark for the rest of the night.

"You're the best," Jennifer crooned. I've never met a man like you before in my life, Mark. You turn me on and make me weak in my knees."

Tonight brought back memories, Jennifer thought while she's lying beside Mark. He was inept to making love or satisfying the sexual needs of a woman. No foreplay, no desired words, nothing, just get a hard-on and pumped away, heading to his satisfaction with no concern for the woman orgasm.

Tonight she wondered if she persuade him to try and change his lovemaking technique. But, that didn't happened.

Jennifer faked tonight orgasm with moaning sounds of "Oh Mark, yes, yes, I'm all wet, you feel so big."

The phone rang and woke Jennifer. It's eight am Sunday she answered the call.

"Hello," Jennifer said in a husky voice."Morning mother."

"You're still in bed?" her mother asked.

"Yes. Mariam had her party last night, and I took Monica with me."

"Then, you won't be going to church this morning?"

"I'm still sleepy, think I'll go back to bed."

"All right then, I'll call you later today," her mother said before hanging up the phone.

Jennifer went back into the bedroom and woke Mark.

"Mark. That was my mother on the phone, you have to get up and leave, she's on her way over here." She lied.

"I thought we'll go out for brunch later this morning, knowing I'll be flying out tomorrow," Mark said sitting on the edge of the bed.

"It's too late now, my mother will soon be here."

Mark got dressed and left Jennifer's house. A few moments after he left, Jennifer got back into her bed and slept peacefully. She was no longer concerned about Mark.

Sleeping with him had been a mistake, Jennifer already know what he was like in bed, but now he'd be going away to America, a farewell gift.

Jennifer wasn't sure if meeting him at the party was coincidence, she wondered what had happened to changed him, Mark's behavior was so unlike him, maybe his wife did left him.

Barbados Heroine

Chapter 9

Monica got out of bed at six am and went to Miami Beach for an early morning swim. She walked along the water's edge while the tide rushed onto the sand, ten minutes down, turned, and walked ten minutes back.

~ ~ ~

Back in London, Alex Smith visited his friend to return his wheels after using the car for the recent date he had the previous night. While he's there, Theodore Williams's cell phone buzzed. He answered and chatted when Alex went into the kitchen and grabbed a beer from the fridge.

"What sounds like a plan?" Alex asked, wandering in from the kitchen.

"You eavesdropping on me now?" Theodore responded. "Listening to my conversation?"

"No. But you will tell me, anyway."

"You raid my fucking fridge and didn't bring me one of my beers?"

Theodore asked, putting away the cell phone.

"Here, take this. I'll fetch another one for myself," Alex said, offering the beer to Theodore.

"Tell me about the hot date you had with Lauren Alleyne!"

"She's hot stuff," Alex replied. "Where's Jasmine? I thought she was staying the entire weekend with you?"

"Jasmine received a call late last night from someone about today, she left early this morning to go back home."

"Okay."

"You will see Lauren again?" Theodore asked.

"We couldn't keep our hands off each other."

"Good for you, buddy," Theodore replied. "What about your online connections?"

"Don't know. What about you? What are you going to do with your own?"

"That was an online hookup I was chatting with earlier."

Barbados Heroine

"What's the plan for today?"

"Her name is Kelly Chatham. She was telling me how horny she was and what she'll do to me when we get together."

"When are you planning to see her?"

"Who said I will meet with her?"

"Oh. I thought that's what you were planning earlier on the phone."

"She's planning on us getting together next weekend."

"What about Jasmine? She's with you every weekend since the two of you started dating."

"I know. I have to come up with a plausible excuse."

"Where's she living?"

"She lives in Middlesex, about a twenty-minute drive from my home."

"Why don't you meet her there?"

"Think I'll suggest that to her. Alex, she sent me a video. She's leaning on a chair and her ass is rolling, talk about movements."

"And you want to sample what she's got."

"Yes. I can't get her ass out of my mind, the way she moves it makes me think about what it would be like to sample it."

"You think she'd go for a threesome?"

"Don't know. The next time I talk with her, I'll drop a hint and get her reaction," Theodore promised. "What will you be doing next weekend?"

"Lauren's birthday will be on Thursday. She wants me to take her to the casino."

"Didn't you tell her you're not a gambler?"

"I buy lottery tickets, I guess that makes me a gambler of some sort."

"I'm talking about poker and slot machines."

"I know what you're saying," Alex shrugged.

"Does Lauren play the slots online?"

"I don't know."

"You have the remaining days of the week to find out."

Monday morning, a phone call from her father got Monica out of bed.

"Hello. good morning," Monica said.

"Did I wake you? I know it's early there, but I thought you should know right away."

"What's going on Dad?"

"The trial is due to start on Thursday."

"Thursday?"

"Yes. The Chief Crown Prosecutor called this morning and informed us that the date was set for this coming Thursday. I told him you were in Barbados, and he said that he would appreciate it very much if you could attend."

"I'll be there. I want justice for Joseph. That Blasted terrorist stabbed Joseph because he wanted to kill someone, anyone. He didn't care who it was."

"Yes. Joseph was in the wrong place at the wrong time."

"Have the Chief Crown Prosecutor mentioned anything about Joseph's parents. Are they going to be there?"

"The Crown Prosecutor mentioned nothing to me."

"Justice for Joseph is all I want."

"I know you do. What about your project? Don't they need you there?" Rosevelt raised a brow.

"No, they don't, and I believe it will be ready to open ahead of schedule," Monica assured her father. "How is my mother?"

"Hold on, she's here," Rosevelt said while handing the phone to his wife Sybil.

"Monica. How are you? How's the weather down there?" Sybil delightfully asked.

"I am good. The weather here's the same, it rains for ten minutes then the sun comes out for the remainder of the day."

"It's cloudy here the last few days, we haven't seen the sun, and it's chilly at night. Are you coming back for the trial?"

"Yes, mother. I'll try to be there on Thursday," Monica promised and continued. "Is Stephany at home?"

"No. She went to her office early this morning."

"Okay, mother. I'll book a flight and let you know what time I'll be arriving in London."

"Goodbye. I'll let Stephany and Theodore

know that you called."

"Goodbye, mom," Monica cheerfully said before hanging up the phone.

Monica then called Virgin Atlantic Airways office in Barbados and booked a seat on the first available flight from Barbados to London Gatwick Airport, United Kingdom. The flight date was the following Wednesday, which gives her one more day on the Island.

Monica then called her parents to inform them about her date and time of arrival at Gatwick.

"Hello," Rosevelt said when he answered the phone.

"Dad. My flight's book for Wednesday on Virgin Atlantic Airlines."

"Okay. I'll pick you up at Gatwick Airport."

"Thank, dad. Please let mom and the others know that I'll see them later this week!"

"Yes. I will let them know you'll be back on Wednesday."

"See you soon dad."

"Safe flight!" her dad wished her.

Monica hung up the phone and gathered a few personal items that she'll need for the flight back to the UK. Her passport and other identification documents. The call brought back memories of her fiance.

During her days at the University, she meet and fell in love with Joseph Gibbs who was also studying Literature at the same University.

Barbados Heroine

Joseph Gibbs was the only child of Brandon Gibbs and Veronica Ryan/Gibbs.

Brandon Gibbs was a Jamaica entertainer and owner of the West Indian music shop, specializing in music from the Caribbean Islands.

Veronica Ryan/Gibbs was a high school teacher, and an author in children books.

Brandon Gibbs, not only was he bringing West Indian music to London, but also the herb known as Marijuana.

One evening, Joseph return home from school and found his mother laying on the floor bleeding from a bullet wound. He tried to reach his dad at the store, but couldn't, then he dial 999.

The house was searched, papers and books were thrown about the floor, dresser drawers were left opened.

Paramedics arrived, so did a couple of police officers. The medics after examine the body concluded that the woman was dead. The M/E was called to the scene and the Chief inspector.

Peter Morrissy had been appointed Camden's (DCI) Detective Chief Inspector several months ago, and this was his first homicide.

"What do we have George?" inspector Morrissy asked the M/E.

"We have a dead woman."

"How long?"

"Many hours ago, I'll know more when I examine the body back at the morgue," the M/E stated.

"Who was the first officer on the scene?" the inspector asked aloud.

"I was sir," a young officer said.

"Any one else was in the house when you arrived?"

"Yes, the dead woman son, he's the one that made the 999 call."

"Where is he?"

"He's outside sitting in a squad car. Would you like to talk with him, sir?"

"Yes."

"Should I go and get him?"

"No. I'll go and talk to him outside, I don't want him to look at his mother laying on the floor like that again." Morrissy continued."What about the husband, his father?"

"Sergeant Everton is on his way to the family store to get the husband as we speak," replied the officer. "The boy said he called the store, but couldn't reach his dad."

DCI Morrissy gaze at the officer with a look of concern on his face. At that moment his cell phone buzzed.

"Morrissy here," he said.

"You have to come and see this," Sergeant Everton said.

"What's the address?" Morrissy asked, then he listen to the sergeant for the address and directions.

"I'm on my way."the inspector said, then turned off his phone.

Inside the store was a mess, items were scattered everywhere.

"What happened here?" the inspector asked when the sergeant approached him.

"The sign on the store front said close, but the car was parked beside the building. I walked around to the back, kicked the door in and found the owner with a bullet hole at the back of his scull," sergeant Everton said leading the inspector to the smashed in back door.

"Did you touch anything other?"

"No. The bullet was in full view."

"We'll wait for the M/E. Clear everyone out of here!" Morrissy commanded.

The M/E preliminary finding was that, the husband and wife was shot around the same time or a few minutes apart.

The murders was never solved.

"I never, ever going to do that again," Stephany groaned, while the gym assistant helped her put the barbells back into the stand.

"You added too much weight on the bar," the gym assistant said to her.

"Yes. I guess it was a little too much for me," Stephany agreed while getting off the workout bench.

After Oliver Compton accepted the offer from his company to take over the Australian branch,

Stephany only received two messages in the six months Oliver's been away.

Stephany thought about Oliver when she left the gym, got into her car, and drove away while her cell phone rang.

"Hello," Stephany said.

"Where are you?" Lolita asked.

"Now leaving the gym. What's up?"

"I'm at the office. I came in early to catch up on some mail I didn't finish yesterday."

"That's why you call me?"

"I came across an interesting email from someone in the United States."

"I'll be at the office in about an hour, we'll go over it then," Stephany said before turning off the cell phone.

One week earlier, Stephany moved out of her parents' home and into a newly renovated flat. The flat was in a Victorian-style house and closer to her office.

From the outside, it wasn't pretty and neither elegant, but Stephany knew her flat would look very nice when she's finished with the decoration.

Boxes were still laying on the floor, filled with items. With her big sister Monica coming back to London next week for the trial of the man who killed her fiance. Stephany thought her sister would help her with the decorating of her new flat.

Stephany took a shower, got dressed, and headed for the office.

Barbados Heroine

During the drive, Stephany's mind was darting around wondering who could've sent the email Lolita had mentioned.

"Who sent the email?" Stephany asked Lolita while taking off her suit jacket and hanging it over the back of her chair.

"It's from Mr. Mark Cornwell."

Stephany opened her PC and the emails and read the one from Mark Cornwell.

The email read. " Mss Williams/ Greaves. I came across a copy of your magazine today, and notice that the printing is done in the United Kingdom. I am wondering if you have ever considered the possibility to have the printing for the United States done here in America? I would appreciate having a forum with you about such a venture. I look forward to hearing from you soon."

"What do you think?" Lolita asked after they finish reading the email.

"I know that having an office in America will be a significant asset to our company, not only the printing of the magazine but a place for taking orders and distributing," Stephany shrugged.

"Yeah. We talked about doing that before, I think the time is here to set up the office in America."

"Do you have any idea of where we should have this office? I mean what state?"

"No," Lolita replied.

"What about Florida?"

"They are so many places we could set-up. Los Angeles, New York, Chicago."

"If we decide on Florida, I can ask my uncle Otis about the best location to have our office. He's been living there for many years and has a company there."

"Why don't you contact him with the information and get his response!" Lolita suggest.

"You agree on Florida?"

"We have to start somewhere, Florida is as good a place as any."

"Kool," Stephany said. "Let's do a night on the town, it's been awhile since we did a girl's night out."

"Yes, let's," Lolita agreed.

Barbados Heroine

Chapter 10

For some time Stephany Williams had been thinking about taking a lover. She finally decided to do something about her love life. The man she'd been dating had moved to Australia, and she hadn't heard from him in quite a long time. The night on the town, Stephany and Lolita out of the office, they chatted about what's going on in their love life while sitting at a corner table in the restaurant with a bottle of red wine.

"I have to find a sex shop, I need something for when I wake up in the middle of the night and have the urge," Lolita explained.

"There's a store in Battersea, or you can go online and find a sex toy shop if you don't want to go to the one in Battersea," Stephany suggested.

"Some nights I feel like having something huge up in there," Lolita said with a facial expression.

They laughed and took a sip of wine from their glasses.

"What about you? How are you coping knowing that Oliver won't be coming back to you?" Lolita asked.

"Some days are bad, some are better," Stephany shrugged.

"You remember Jimmy? He's one of Olivers' friends. I was on Facebook two days ago and he had the nerve to send me a friend request."

"Maybe Oliver told him he's not dating you anymore."

"It's possible. I think they are good friends from school days."

"Did you accept the friend request? Or deleted it?"

"I removed it."

"Delete them if you don't want to be a friend on Facebook."

"Yes. I know." Lolita changed the subject.

"Do you know the address of the sex shop in Battersea?" she asked.

"I went there once with Oliver. He went to get

oil and gave me a full body massage," Stephany sighed and closed her eyes. "It felt so good, I can remember him doing things to me after the massage I never thought I would ever encounter."

"Girl, you got me thinking of some kinky shit right now. You know, I've seen some of those batteries-operated ones.

"You going to get one of those and try it?"

"I'm thinking about it, listening to you talking about massages got me feeling for some kinky shit," Lolita said while giggling.

"Come on! Let's go to the sex shop and get your toys."

"That way, I'll be ready for anything any man wants to try with me, No part of my body will be a virgin anymore."

Wednesday afternoon, Monica Williams boarded the Virgin Atlantic Airlines flight to London, UK.

Monica passed through customs and immigration with no problems. Her dad Rosevelt was waiting for her at the Arrival Terminal.

"How was your flight?" her dad asked while taking the carry-on bag from Monica.

"I listen to music and slept a little," Monica shrugged her shoulder.

"Your sister has moved out. She found a flat closer to her office."

"When did she moved?" Monica responded.

"About two weeks ago."

"How did mom take it?" Monica asked, highly intrigued.

"She put up a good front by helping Stephany packed her things, but I know she was hurting inside seeing her last remaining child who's living at home pack up and go."

"Now it'll only be the two of you living in that sizeable house. Have you thought about downsizing and getting a smaller place for you and mom?" Monica asked while raising a brow.

"We've never discussed moving, but not that everyone has moved out, we will give it some thought, although I don't think your mother will want to give up the house, hoping one of you will move back home."

"Her thoughts would be of Stephany and Theodore. She knows I'll be living in Barbados."

"Stephany Just moved out, I don't think she'll be moving back home anytime soon, and besides, she and her co-founder are thinking about opening a branch in the United States."

"Okay, dad. What about your mistress? Or should I say, mistresses?"

"What?" Rosevelt raised his voice a notch.

"Oh, you think I didn't know about them!"

Rosevelt continues driving without a response.

"Come on dad. It's only you and I here in the car."

"Anyone else knows about it? And how long have you known?" Rosevelt enquired.

Barbados Heroine

"I suspected it a long time ago with something I saw at the store. And to my knowledge, no one else at home knows about it," Monica replied.

"Your mother and I will always love each other, we'll never split up. Since she had the operation to remove her thyroids, things changed in the bedroom."

"Mom and I didn't have any girl talk since the operation."

"We'll continue this conversation before you leave to go back to Barbados," her dad suggested while pulling into the driveway and stopping the car.

Her mother Sybil was standing on the steps with the front door open when Monica got out of the car.

"Hello mother," Monica whispered in Sybil's ear while they hugged each other.

"How was your flight?"

"I slept a little," Monica responds with a shrug of her shoulder while she followed her mother into the house.

Rosevelt took Monica's carry-on bag from the back seat of the car and followed Sybil and Monica into the house after closing the front door behind him.

"Are you hungry?" her mother asked when they sat down on the couch in the living room.

"I had a snack on board the plane."

"A snack! I prepared your favorite meal of

spare-ribs, baked macaroni-pie, with a cucumber salad. Come on and eat something!" her mother suggested.

Rosevelt took the carry-on bag to Monica's bedroom, then returned and join his wife and daughter.

"Have you heard from Theodore recently?" Monica asked her parents.

"Yes, he called earlier today and said he'll be coming over tomorrow," her mother replied.

~ ~ ~

At seven o'clock on Thursday morning, Monica woke up to the buzzing of her cell phone. She picked it up from the nightstand.

"Hello," Monica said into the receiver.

"Hi Sis," Stephany said. "Did I wake you?"

"Yeah, you did. But that's okay, I have to be up and get myself ready to go to the hearing at the courthouse."

"What time do you have to be there?"

"The Crown Prosecutor asked me to be there for eight-thirty," Monica responded highly intrigued.

"Is dad going with you?"

"He didn't say, and I haven't ask."

"I can take some time off and go with you," Stephany suggested.

"Great, I'll like that."

Barbados Heroine

"Okay. I'll let Lolita know that I'm going with you this morning to the courthouse and will be at the office in the afternoon."

"I'll be ready when you get here."

"See you soon," Stephany said before turning off her cell phone.

At eight o'clock, Stephany picked up Monica, and they went to the courthouse.

The assistant Crown Prosecutor meets them on the steps of the trial room.

"Good morning, Misses Williams," he greeted them with an outstretched hand.

"Good morning, Mr. Berkley," Monica said while shaking his hand. Stephany did likewise.

"We have a few minutes before the trial starts, let me bring you up to date on what will happen today. Follow me," he said while turning and headed for an empty conference room.

Monica and Stephany followed the Crown Prosecutor into the vacant conference room.

A long table with five leather chairs on each side occupied the room.

"Yesterday I received a call from the Defense-Barrister representing Mr. Khaled Salem informing me that his client is going to plea guilty to the charges brought against him," the Prosecutor said, taking a folder from his briefcase.

"What does this mean?" Stephany asked curiously.

"It means there won't be a trial by jury. The

judge will ask a few questions to make sure that Mr. Salem understood what will happen. The judge will then remand him into custody and set a date for the sentencing."

"How long will that take?" Monica asked eagerly.

"Come on! Let us go to the courtroom," The Prosecutor suggested.

Monica and Stephany entered the trial room with the Crown Prosecutor and sat down in the seats behind him.

The hearing didn't take long. Forty-five minutes later, Monica and Stephany left the courthouse and drove back to their parents' home.

"How did it go?" their mother asked when they entered the house.

"Salem pleaded guilty to the charge of first-degree murder, the judge will pass his sentence one week from today," Monica explained to her mother.

"Did you have to do or say anything?"

"No. We sat in the seats behind the Prosecutor, that's all we did," Monica said while tears flowed from her eyes.

The three women then form a group hug.

"There, there, everything will be all right," her mother said to Monica while they continued to hug each other, Stephany then started sobbing too.

"We all miss Joseph, and now justice will be served upon his killer," Sybil said, raising her voice a notch.

"Let's all go out for lunch," Stephany suggested after composing herself.

"Are you up to it, Monica?" her mother asked.

"Yes. I'll freshen up a bit, then we'll go," Monica responded while wiping tears away from her eyes.

Minutes later, Monica, Stephany, and their mother got into Stephany's car and headed to lunch.

At the buffet restaurant, they were ushered to a table by the window.

"Mother. Do you want me to prepare a plate for you?" Stephany asked after they sat down at the table.

"No, I'll choose what I want."

"Are we going to have a bottle of wine?" Stephany asked.

"Mom, do you want to have a glass of wine?" Monica inquired while getting up from the table.

"Whatever you girls decide is okay with me," their mother replied when she got up and went to the buffet table with Monica, leaving Stephany to order the drinks.

Monica and her mother took chicken wings, steam veggies, egg rolls, and went back to the table. Stephany took ribs with veg fried rice, egg rolls, and veggies. She ordered a bottle of Bordeaux to go with their lunch.

After they finished lunch, Stephany drove her

mother and sister back to the house and then went to her office.

"How did it go?" Lolita asked Stephany when she entered the office.

"The killer pleaded guilty to the charges, the judge will pass judgment next week."

"Monica must be happy."

"Seeing the killer again brought back terrible memories for her, so I took mom and her to lunch."

"Cool."

"How are things here? What did I miss?" Stephany asked.

"One complaint from Mac's bookstore. He said that he's running of this month's copies."

"Did you notify shipping?"

"Yes, they'll deliver the order to Mac's bookstore later today."

"Great. Now, tell me all about it!"

"Tell you about what?"

"You know, the latest addition to your bedroom items."

"Girl, let me tell you. I gave myself a good fucking last night, I can't remember cumming so much, and that small part of it, tickle my ass so good, for the first time in my life I felt like having something up in there," Lolita replied while squeezing her legs together.

"So, why didn't you try using the bigger side and see if it would go in?"

Barbados Heroine

"It felt so good in my cunt, I didn't want to take it out, and then later I felt so weak after cumming so much that I fall asleep, maybe next time I'll try."

"That's why you look so refresh today."

"You should get one of those things for yourself and give your puss a workout?" Lolita suggested shrugging her shoulders with a grin on her face.

"I was waiting to hear your report on how it made you feel, now, I may get one."

"We can go after work," Lolita said.

The next day was Friday, and Monica had no plans of doing much for the weekend. She decided she'll take her mother Sybil for a walk around the Clapham Common and the public park for an early morning workout.

Eight o'clock, Monica got out of bed, went to the bathroom, brush her teeth, then went to the kitchen where her mother was preparing a pot of coffee.

"Good morning mother," Monica said putting a hand on her mother's shoulder and kissing her.

"Did you have a good sleep?"

"Yes, I did. Where's dad?"

"He already left to go to the store."

"Okay. How about going for a walk this morning?"

"That's a good idea," Sybil agreed.

"We'll have a coffee and go for a walk, then

eat breakfast when we return home," Monica suggested while pouring two cups of coffee.

The walk around the Clapham Common and the park took Monica and her mother, Sybil, one hour to complete before returning home.

After a healthy breakfast of cereal and fruits, Monica asks her mother.

"What are we going to do today?"

"I'll leave that up to you," Sybil replied, shrugging her shoulder.

"How about going to Hay's Galleria Shopping Mall, then we could go by the store and have lunch with dad?touch,"

"What time you want to leave?" her mother asked.

"After we freshen up, we can leave whenever you're ready."

"Okay."

Once in her bedroom, Monica punched in the numbers for the store. Her dad finally answered after three attempts.

"Hello," he said after putting the receiver to his ear.

"Hey, dad. What's going on? You took a long time to answer the phone, I was about to think something has happened."

"No. Everything is okay. I was taking inventory on some items that are going out of stock."

"I'm calling to let you know that we are going

to the shopping mall, and when we're finished, we will come to the store and have lunch with you."

"Great. I'm looking forward to seeing you girls."

Lunch at Roberto's, a restaurant perched overlooking the Thames River, was suitable for the occasion. Monica and her mother shared a huge seafood platter of lobster, shrimp, and crab legs, while Rosevelt had the chicken and ribs combo. They ordered a bottle of Chardonnay.

Everything was perfect for the family lunch outing. Monica smiled and pretended she didn't notice how her dad and mom looked at each other as they ate lunch.

After lunch, Monica and her mother went home, and Rosevelt went back to the store.

Chapter 11

Soon after returning home, Monica's cell phone rang.

"Hello. Sis," she said after seeing Stephany's name displayed on the screen.

"What's up?" Stephany asked.

"Mom and I not long got back from having lunch with dad."

"Cool. Where did you go?"

"We went to Roberto's."

"Nice. I haven't been there in a long time."

"What's up with you?"

"Not much. You want to come over and see

my place later this evening after I finish work?"

"Yup."

"I'll pick you up on my way home."

"Okay, see you later. You want to chat with mom?"

"Not really, I'll see her when I come to pick you up."

Friday evening, Stephany picked up her sister at their parent's home and drove to her flat.

"What do you think?" Stephany asked after she and Monica entered the flat.

Monica walked through the apartment, avoiding the cardboard boxes on the floor.

"It's very nice. I like it," Monica replied.

"Great. Then you'll help me this weekend with decorating it?"

"Yes."

"Theodore promised to come by on Saturday," Stephany said, shrugging her shoulders.

"He's not chasing girls this weekend?" Monica inquired.

"Theodore has been acting more matured since he began dating a woman named Jasmine Howell, who is much older than him."

"If she's making him happy, then it doesn't matter if she's older," Monica stated, raising a brow.

"That's what I told him when he asked my opinion about the age difference."

"Will he bring her on Saturday?"

"Yes. Theodore would like you to meet her."

"Cool."

"I have a bottle of white wine in the fridge. Do you want a glass?"

"I drank a glass of Chardonnay at lunch today," Monica said. "Maybe later."

"Where should we start?"

"Let's do the living room first," Monica replied.

Stephany opened the box containing the curtains and began hanging them on the living room windows.

"What about that boyfriend of yours?" Monica asked.

"We broke up. Or should I say, he broke up with me," Stephany stupes and shrug a shoulder.

"What happened? I didn't know," Monica said. "You can tell me all about it."

"Not much to tell. The company offered him a position at the office in Australia, and he took it. We stayed in touch, then suddenly he stopped returning my texts. I believed he's found a woman over there."

"I'm sorry, sis."

"Don't be. It didn't work out for us."

"You'll find someone who is tall, dark, handsome, and rich," Monica said.

The sisters looked at each other and laughed.

"What about you?" Stephany asked. "Have you found anyone in Barbados?"

Barbados Heroine

"No. My mind is on getting the business started, although I went to one party and saw some fine-looking men in attendance."

"What about Randolph? have you heard anything from him?"

"No. I will call Randolph tomorrow, not sure if he's in town or touring with the club."

"Okay. Let's take a break and have a glass of wine," Stephany suggested.

"Good idea."

"How about some cheese and crackers, I also have grapes and strawberries."

"Great," Monica replied while heading for the washroom to wash her hands. "How's Lolita doing?"

"Girl, let me tell you, she's something else. She went to the sex shop and bought this dildo with an extra piece on it and told me she gave herself a good fucking, saying it made her cum multiple times."

"Did Lolita buy a battery operate one?"

"Yes, she did."

"Did you buy one for yourself?"

"No, I didn't."

"Two sisters, and not one of us has a man," Monica stated.

Monica and Stephany looked at each other and took a sip of wine.

Monica woke at 11.00 am, took a shower, and then joined Stephany in the kitchen.

"Morning sis," Stephany greeted Monica when she sat down at the kitchen table.

"Morning to you too," Monica replied.

"Did you have a good sleep?"

"Yes, I did."

"Theodore called earlier."

"Is he still coming over?"

"Yes. Theodore and his girlfriend will be here around noon."

Monica punched in the numbers for Randolph Channing's mobile phone and waited for an answer. The call went directly to voice-mail. Monica turned off her cell after hearing that the mailbox was full.

At 12.30 pm, the doorbell to Stephany's flat rang. "Who is it," Stephany enquired through the intercom.

"It's Theodore Sis," her brother replied from outside the door.

Stephany buzzed him into the building, then opened the door to her flat and waited for Theodore.

Carrying a brown paper bag in each hand, they greeted each other with a hug and a kiss on both cheeks.

"This is Jasmine," Theodore said, handing the two bags to Stephany. "I have to go back to the car."

"Come in, Jasmine," Stephany instructed. "My big sister is in the living room, come and meet her."

Jasmine entered the flat carrying one brown paper bag in her hand. She followed Stephany into the living room where Monica was standing on a ladder, hanging pictures on the wall.

"Monica, this is Jasmine, your brother's girlfriend," Stephany said while taking the bag from Jasmine.

Monica got down from the small step-ladder and greeted Jasmine with a hug.

"You are beautiful," Monica said, giving Jasmine a look of admiration.

"Thank you," Jasmine responded while blushing. "And I must Theodore have two beautiful sisters."

The buzzer to the flat went off.

"That must be Theodore, he went to the car to get something," Stephany said while heading for the door.

"He went back to the car for the case of beer," Jasmine informs them.

"Something in those bags smells good," Monica said.

"We picked up four take away portions of food, vegetable fried rice with chicken, a vegetable platter with fish and two rice and peas with BBQ ribs," Jasmine said.

Theodore entered the flat with a six-pack of beer and a bottle of Rose wine. He put the items down on the kitchen table, then went to his sister

Monica.

"Well, sis. What do you think?" Theodore asked while hugging Monica.

"Think about what?"

"What do you think about Jasmine?"

"I think you have your hands full," Monica replied. "She's gorgeous and has an impressive body."

"I'm glad you like her," Theodore stated.

"Is everyone ready to eat?" Stephany shouted from the kitchen while putting the beers and wine in the refrigerator.

"After I finish hanging the pictures on the wall, I will have a bite to eat," Monica said from the living room.

"What are you going to do with these empty cardboard boxes?" Theodore asked while gathering them up.

"You can take them out to the recycle bin," Stephany suggested.

"You will keep none of them?"

"No," Stephany replied with a shrug.

Theodore and Jasmine began taking the empty boxes apart, then took the cardboard outside to the bin.

One hour later, the four of them sat down at the kitchen table and ate the food Theodore and Jasmine had brought to the flat.

"What's up?" Stephany asked over the phone Sunday afternoon.

Barbados Heroine

"What's up is I'm knee-deep in vegetables preparing the family Sunday meal which you were to help me with," her mother Sybil answered, cradling the phone under her chin.

"So sorry. Mom, We'll come over."

"Okay."

"Do you need anything else?" Stephany asked. "Wine or soft drinks?"

"No, your father went out to buy the drinks."

Stephany put down the phone after her mother hung up.

"Sis. That was our mother on the phone. We have to go over right away. I'm supposed to be helping her with preparing the family meal this Sunday."

"You forgot."

"Yes, I did," Stephany stated.

"Do you know if Theodore is going to mom's for supper?"

"I'm not sure Theodore said nothing about going to mom's for supper before he left last night."

"Let's go!" commanded Monica, going through the front door of the flat.

Chapter 12

The next day, the city was back at work. Monica took her mother Sybil to the saloon for a mother and daughter haircut, manicure, and pedicure.

Monday night and they were going to the black actor's workshop to watch their latest play.

The next few days, Monica spent quality time with her mother, then after the judge handed down his verdict on her fiance killer on Thursday, Monica took the first flight on Friday morning to Barbados.

"Hi, Theodore," Alex said, opening the front

door to his flat, munching on an apple. Standing behind him was a tall brunette with a statuesque figure and full lips. She wore white shorts, a tank top, and a blank expression. Alex did not introduce her to Theodore. "Stephany stopped by here looking for you," he said, taking a bite on the apple.

"She was?" Theodore said.

"Stephany said she couldn't reach you on your cell, you better call her, she's worried about something."

"I'll do that," Theodore promise. "What's with the new girl. Who's she?"

"You don't remember her. She was one class behind us at school. I saw her at the mall and invited her for a drink, she didn't want to go to the bar, so we ended up here at my place."

"I thought you and Lauren were hooking up this weekend?"

"No, she canceled. Something about a family getting together for a going away party."

Theodore punched in Stephany's cell phone number. She answered after the second attempt.

"Where have you been?" Stephany asked.

"I spent the night at Jasmine's place. What's up? Alex said you looked worried about something."

"I couldn't reach you. Then, I tried to reach my friend Lolita and didn't. Of course, I am worried."

"Where are you now?"

"I'm heading to Lolita's flat."

"Anything you want me to do?"

"No. We'll chat later."

"Okay," Theodore replied, then turned off his cell phone.

Arriving at Lolita's flat, Stephany found the front gate to the building open. She entered and rang the bell to Lolita's flat after a few moments, Stephany knocked on the door.

"Who is it?" Lolita asked through the intercom system.

"It's me," Stephany replied.

Lolita buzzed the door open to let her in, then sat down on the couch.

"Are you alright?" Stephany asked, after entering the flat and seeing Lolita sitting on the sofa hugging a cushion.

"What time is it?" Lolita asked.

"It's eleven thirty. I was thinking we could do lunch today," Stephany said.

"I don't feel so good," Lolita stated.

"Did you go out last night?"

"Do you remember one of my old boyfriends Brian? He called me last night saying he was in town for the night and wanted to see how I was doing."

"So, after all this time, he suddenly cares about what you're doing?"

"He wanted me to meet him, but I didn't feel like going out, so I invited him over. We drank wine, and we smoked a marijuana joint. It knocked me out, I remember little after that," Lolita said.

"Did you have sex with him?"Stephany asked.

"No, we didn't."

"Where's Brian staying?"

"He's staying at his cousin's house."

"Are you going to see him again today?"

"We didn't talked about hooking up today, at least I don't remember," Lolita shrugged.

"And you're sure no sex were involved?"

"Yes, I'm sure."

~ ~ ~

Saturday morning, Monica punched in the numbers for Jennifer's cell phone.

The call went directly to voice mail. Monica left a message informing Jennifer that she was back in Barbados and to get in touch as soon as possible.

Monica then called her aunt Evelyn James.

"Hello," Evelyn said, answering on the second buzz.

"Hi, auntie," Monica said. "Just letting you know that I'm back on the Island, and to see how you and the family are doing."

"Everyone is doing okay."

"I dial Jennifer's cell phone number but didn't reach her."

"She went to Trinidad for the weekend."

"Okay," Monica said.

"Jennifer often returns on Sunday's afternoon flight," Evelyn informed Monica.

"Are you making pudding and souse today? I'll like a share."

"Yes, always on Saturdays. I'll save you a portion."

"Great."

"Your other cousin Norma will bring it for you this afternoon."

"Mom and dad send their love to you and the rest of the family."

"How are they?" Evelyn asked.

"They are all good."

"Will you be staying at home all day?"

"Yes. I will let you know if I decide to go out." Monica stated.

"Norma will arrive at your house around 1 pm."

"Okay, I'll be here."

"Talk with you later," Evelyn said before hanging up the receiver.

Monica dial the building contractor Sydney Crichlow's phone number. He immediately answered the phone.

"Hello, Miss Williams," he said, seeing her name displayed on the screen of his cell phone.

"Hello, Mr. Crichlow."

"When did you return?"

"I came back yesterday. I will come down to

see the building tomorrow and was wondering if you could meet me there?"

"Of course, I will meet you at the building site."

"Shall we say about eleven o'clock in the morning?" Monica suggested.

"Eleven in the morning would be fine," Sydney Crichlow replied.

Norman Adams's older sister to Jennifer is the manager of their dad's George Adams liquor store, which specializes in exquisite wines.

Norma and Jennifer's parents never got married. When the girls were born, their father George was married to Olivia Jenkins.

George Adams is the owner and CEO of Adams's real estate agency, with offices in Barbados, Trinidad, and Grenada.

George visited these offices regularly. It was on one of these visits to Trinidad when his daughter Jennifer traveled with him and meet her lover, Victor Hernandez.

It was sex at first sight then. She found out he was married, but that didn't stop her from continuing to see him.

George, at the age of sixty-two, has a body of a thirty-something man because of his steady workout exercises.

George has become a middle-aged playboy, rumored to have a female companion in each of the Islands where he has offices.

Norman Adams never stopped having her mother pudding and souse for lunch on Saturday.

Norma always closes the liquor store at noon on Saturdays, giving her staff of three employees the afternoon off.

Today, she will have lunch with her cousin Monica at her residence.

One pm, Norma rang the doorbell at Monica's residence.

"Coming," Monica replied.

"It's me, Norma."

"Come on in!" Monica said.

Norma entered the house and placed the plastic bag containing the two servings of pudding and souse on the kitchen table.

"Do you care to have a drink?" Monica asked.

"A beer if you have."

"Banks or Deputy? I have both."

"Banks, please."

"I'm going to have a Rum and Coke," Monica said. "Are we going to eat now?"

"I am famished," Norma explained.

Monica took out two plates along with forks and spoons and put them on the table after giving Norma the Banks beer.

"I would like you to supply the hotel with alcoholic beverages when needed?" Monica said.

It surprised Norma at the request from Monica. "I've never done that before. Yes, I don't see why not," Norma replied with a shrug of her shoulder.

"After I've hired the food and beverage personnel, we'll get together and supply a list of what we will need from you."

"You know, my mom can help you with the food section, she's good at planning menus, and she has catered to many large and important parties held here on the Island."

"Yes, I'll ask for her input along with the food personnel in planning the menus for the opening party. Our food menus will differ from typical Island cuisine."

Sunday morning, Monica walked to Miami beach and have an early morning stroll along the beach and a swim. On her way back home, she went to the Oistins bus depot and bought copies of the Barbados Nation and Advocate newspaper.

After reaching home, Monica took a shower to wash off the salt from the seawater, then she made a cup of tea, sat down, and looked for the ads about the opening of her establishment.

The ad contained the application form for employment and contact information.

Monica then checked her email and found many people had filled out the online employment application form.

She replied to the applicants with a date and time from their interviews.

Ten thirty, Monica got dressed and leave home to join the building contractor at the site.

Mr. Crichlow was waiting for Monica when she got to the building and parked her car.

Mr. Crichlow walked over and opened the car door.

"Morning, Miss Adams," the contractor said.

"Good morning, Mr. Crichlow."

"Lovely morning," Sydney Crichlow observed.

"Yes, it is."

"We are weeks ahead of the scheduled time we had estimated for the opening," Sydney informs her while they walked through the structure.

"Yes, I see the gardeners are hard at work preparing the soil."

"The roof for the section where you'll be living will go on tomorrow, and the furniture store agent came by last week wanting to know when they can deliver the items for the hotel."

"I will call the decorator this afternoon to find out when she will be available to be here. Then, I'll let the store know when to deliver the furniture."

"Who did you hire to do the decorating?"

"She's a member of the family that does upholstering, refurbishing, and decorating for hotels here on the Island."

After the tour of the two hundred rooms' hotel structure, Monica returned to her home.

Monica punched in the numbers to the decorator Lauren Weeks' cell phone.

Barbados Heroine

"Hello," Lauren said after the third attempt.

"Good afternoon, Lauren. How are you?" Monica asked.

"Hi, Monica. Didn't know you were back in Bim."

"Came back on Friday."

"How's the rest of the family?"

"They're good," Monica replied. "When will you be available to decorate the interior of the hotel?"

"I have finished my latest project. I will be at the hotel starting on Monday."

"You will let me know when you'll be ready to have the furnishing delivered," Monica suggested.

"After I've finished with the windows and floors, I'll let you know what items to have delivered first."

"Any idea how long it's going to take?"

"I'll bring you up to date daily."

"Okay, I will come to the hotel on Monday and see you," Monica promised.

"See you on Monday," Lauren replied, then turned off her phone.

Jennifer returns to Barbados on the three pm flight from Trinidad. On her way home from the airport, Jennifer stopped and visited Monica, who was sitting on a chair on the veranda at the front of the house when Jennifer arrived.

"Hi, Monica," Jennifer said when she got out of the car.

"Hi, Jenn. Did you bring me anything from T & T?" Monica asked, standing up from the chair.

They hugged, then Jennifer and Monica sat down.

"I brought you a head-scarf," Jennifer replied.

"I also brought back something from London for you," Monica said.

"How are the rest of the family in London?"

"Everyone is doing fine. What about your man in Trinidad?"

"I had enough of him, and I told him so when he dropped me off at the airport for my flight home."

"How did he take it?"

"I don't know. I got out of the car at the departure entrance by the time it took him to find parking for the car. I was through the security area where he couldn't enter."

"He didn't message you while you were waiting to board the plane?"

"Yes, he did, but I didn't reply to him."

"Then it's over?"

"Yes. Don't know what I was thinking but, Victor looked so damn handsome when I first saw him I just wanted to fuck him."

"How long were you involved with him?"

"A few years, we travel back and forth on weekends, sometime Victor would visit other times I would go to Trinidad."

"When will you be available to help me with

these applications?"

"Whenever you're ready to start, let me know."

"I've answered a few."

"I'll come up tomorrow evening."

"Cool. What about the interviews? Have you found a place to conduct them?"

"No. I was about to look for an available place when I got the message about the trial in London. Now, I'll wait until the office at the hotel is complete, and conduct the interviews there."

"Oh. I forgot about that. What happened at the trial?" Jennifer asked, somewhat skeptically.

"The killer got life behind bars with no chance of parole," Monica replied with a schug.

"That's great."

"Yes. I'm happy with the results, so is the rest of the family," Monica sighed.

"Well, I'm going to leave you and head home."

"You care for something to eat? A drink before you go?"

"No. I had two drinks on the plane," Jennifer said while getting up and heading to the car.

"Get home safe, and I'll see you tomorrow," Monica advised while walking to the car with Jennifer.

Chapter 13

In the next few weeks, Monica and Jennifer worked tirelessly with interviews and the hire of staff for the hotel.

The date for the opening of Williams Atlantic Shores Resorts & Casino was the second Friday in October.

Invitations went out to dignitaries of the Government and other important people.

On Tuesday morning, the day after the long holiday weekend. The phone at Monica's residence rang.

She picked up the receiver on the second buzz.

Barbados Heroine

"Good morning," Monica said.

"Morning Cousin," the trembling voice on the other end said. "This is Norma."

"Hi Norma, I didn't recognize your voice."

"I have some bad news. There's been a death in the family."

"Oh my God. Who died?" Monica asked curiously.

"A car struck and killed your cousin John Williams while riding his motorcycle on the auto-route last night."

"Any details on how it happened?"

"We heard bits and pieces about the accident. We will know more later today."

"Where is everyone now?"

"Mom and some others went to the hospital. We are going to meet at her place later this afternoon. We know you're busy preparing for the opening of the hotel, so if you can't come, we will understand."

"No. Nonsense, I'm coming."

"After 3 pm is good."

"Okay, I will see you all later," Monica promise.

"Great," Norma said, then hung up the phone.

Monica then called London, England. Her mother Sybil answered the phone.

"Good afternoon," Sybil said.

"Morning, Mom. Oops, I mean afternoon, for a minute I forgot you're 4 hours ahead of us here in

Barbados," Monica said.

"Is everything all right? You sound a little concerned."

"There's a death in the family. I don't know if you know or remember John Williams."

"John, John Williams. Yes, little Johnny, what happened?"

"He was killed last night on the highway while riding his motorcycle."

"So sorry to hear. John is the son of your other uncle, Leroy Williams."

"No one never mentioned Leroy Williams to me."

"If I remember correctly, Leroy died a long time ago from a motorcycle accident when it went over a cliff after the front tire blew out."

"Okay. How's dad and the others?"

"We're all good. We will see you soon. Everyone is coming down for the opening of the hotel."

"Great. I'll see you guys in a few weeks. Let the others know about the death," Monica suggested.

"Of course I will," Sybil promised.

John Williams was a graduate of Louis Lynch Secondary School. At a young age, John loved playing around with anything that had an engine, he knew his calling and decided to become an auto mechanic. He also believed in the school motto.

Barbados Heroine

~ ~ ~

Strength to Strength.

After learning the trade for a few years, John began buying and repairing old cars in his parents backyard. His repair and sell business grew so fast, John got a loan from his bank and bought a auto repair garage that had gone out of business.

Eventually upgrading and expanding the building and went into the automobile dealership business, for new and used vehicles.

John Williams never got married, not that he didn't received many offers.

"I'm not the marrying kind," John would always reply when asked by any one why don't he tie the knot.

John never wanted to get too attached to any woman after he lost the mother of his only son to cancer. He dated many women, that's as far he went with any relationship.

The funeral of John Williams was a solemn affair. It took place in Speightstown in the Parrish of St. Peters on the north-side of the Island.

There were over one hundred mourners gathered at the gravesite. Front and center was John Williams's only son Joseph.

Joseph Williams was a graduate of Coleridge & Parry Secondary School.

Joseph stood with a depressive look on his

face. Later he maintained that same expression as people lined up to offer their condolences.

Joseph recognized most of the men. They were his dad's friends. Some of the women he also recognized from being customers at his dad's Automobile dealership.

"I am sorry," one of the men said, shaking his hand with a firm grip.

"Thank you for coming," Joseph said.

"We'll all miss him," a woman said in a sympathetic voice while shaking Joseph's hand. "He talked about you all the time. John also said that you got yourself a pretty girlfriend."

"He's right. I have,"Joseph replied.

"I'll like to meet her. Having the right girl can help you through times such as this, in your moments of grief."

"I've seen you before, but I can't remember your name."

"My name is Pamela Gooding, a special friend of your dad," the woman explained, then moved along that other mourners can pay their respects.

~ ~ ~

There was a formal reception back at the church in the conference room. Most of the people were content with sitting and eating with someone they already knew instead of mixing with others.

Family members were walking around the

tables, greeting and chatting with the mourners.

Joseph and his girlfriend, Marcia Roberts, also moved around the tables, greeting and chatting while Joseph introduces her to the people he recognized.

Marcia Roberts was also a graduate of Coleridge & Parry School. She stood out in a crowd with her 5' 10" athletic body.

Marcia won many medals taking part in the inter school 100 meters and high jump compctitions until a broken ankle put a stop to her competing in sports.

Marcia Roberts was a lightskinned, curvy woman with curly black hair.

Pamela stood up from her table when Joseph approached.

"Mrs. Gooding, this is my girlfriend, Marcia Roberts," Joseph said with a sad sound in his voice.

"Please to meet you, Marcia," Pamela Gooding said while they shook hands.

"Nice to meet you, Mrs. Gooding," Marcia replied.

"It's Miss, not Mrs," Pamela explained while looking at Joseph.

"I think Pamela Gooding likes you," Marcia said when they turned away from the table.

"She was a special friend of my father's."

"So. I saw the way she looked at you when she said Miss, not Mrs. Gooding."

"I didn't notice," Joseph replied with a schug.

After greeting the people who weren't in the line to offer their sympathy earlier, Joseph and Marcia sat down with the other members of the family and ate a plate of chicken and rice.

Joseph's dad's lawyer was there, a slender man in his early forties wearing a pair of black pants, a grey jacket with cummerbund, and black shoes.

"We have a lot to talk about, young man," the lawyer said, while he taps Joseph on his shoulder to get his attention.

Joseph got up from the table and shook the lawyer's hand.

"We certainly do. You're Mr. Peterson, correct?"

"Yes, I am."

"Must we do that now?" Joseph asked.

"We can set up an appointment. Either you come to my office or, I'll meet you at the dealership," the lawyer explained.

"That would be best."

"There's not much to do. Your dad already has you listed as part-owner of the company. It's only the formality of signing a few documents," Peterson informed Joseph.

"I'm available any day next week. Call me, and let's set a date," Joseph said.

"Sorry for your loss. Your dad was a very respectable man in the community. We will miss him."

Barbados Heroine

"Thank you very much."

Joseph and his girlfriend Marcia were one of the last couples to leave the reception.

Minutes later, they arrived at the house that Joseph shared with his late father.

"Will you stay with me tonight?" he asked Marcia when they entered the house.

For the first time since his dad died, Joseph cried while Marcia hugged him tightly.

"Sure, I will," she whispered. I have to go home, change my clothes, and come back. I will leave here in the morning and go directly to work."

"Maybe you should bring over more than one change of clothes and stay here with me for a few days," Joseph suggests.

"Okay," Marcia agreed while walking to the door. "I'll be back shortly."

"I'm already missing you," Joseph said while he followed Marcia to the door, he watched as she drove away, then went and took a beer from the fridge.

~ ~ ~

Thursday. Williams Atlantic Shores Resort & Casino was abuzz as the first guests checked in one day ahead of the official opening of the hotel.

Monica's family from England and America were among the many people arriving on

Sherwin A Goodman

Thursday.

Stephany had not set foot in Barbados since leaving the place of her birth 23 years ago.

She stepped off the plane and took a deep breath and smiled.

"What are you smiling about?" her brother Theodore asked.

"You were too young to remember. But the place smell the same," Stephany replied.

"You remember the smell after all these years?"

"Yes. It's the salty smell from the ocean," Stephany explained, while they pass through customs and immigration.

Monica was at the airport to meet her family when they got off the plane. She hired a limousine to transport the family from the airport to the hotel.

The airport was doing a roaring business, with many more tourists than usual after they learned about the opening of the first official hotel and casino on the Island.

Fat pot-belly males with young beautiful girls on their arms, other men with plump ladies wearing shorts that were too tight around their waist-line with small children in tow along with their nannies. The tourist season was about to begin on the Island as people from all parts of the globe come to enjoy the warmth of the Caribbean Island of Barbados.

Barbados Heroine

Chapter 14

The Island of Barbados was already known worldwide for its beautiful beaches and hospitality, and was about to attract more high rollers and big spenders in the gambling industry with the opening Williams Atlantic Shores Resort & Casino.

Early Friday morning, there's a knock on Monica's suite door. She opened the door.

"Morning, mother," Monica said when she saw Sybil.

"Did I wake you?" her mother asked.

"No. I woke up a while ago," Monica stated.

"Today is the day."

"Yes, it is a big day for the family."

"And last night was my night."

"Oh? Monica quizzed her mom. "What happened last night?"

"Don't know what got into your father. We drank some wine, and after, he made me feel like a young woman again. Your dad did things to me he hasn't done in a long time."

"That's why you look so refresh, and here I thought it was the Island's atmosphere," Monica said smiling, and kissing Sybil on the cheek.

"Have you had breakfast?" Sybil asked.

"No. Let's take a walk," Monica suggested in an excited voice.

"Where are we going?" Sybil queried.

"I got the urge to walk around our hotel and take it all in before the turmoil starts."

"What turmoil?"

"Guess I'm experiencing that feeling a young child gets before opening their first Xmas gift."

"Happy?"

"Excited, pure excitement."

Monica's dad Rosevelt and her uncle Otis were also up early. The two brothers were out walking along the Atlantic beach and looking out over the ocean.

Jeremy Gordan, the next-door neighbor, was in his routine morning workout of jogging on the beach. This morning was different. He was not alone. Jeremy had brought his New York mistress Gabriel King to the Island for a week-long visit, and the two were now jogging on the beach together.

Visitors who are staying at the hotel were on the beach, enjoying the early morning sunlight and sea-breeze.

Theodore and Stephany were also up early after a late night of partying in the hottest night-spot on the Island.

"What are your plans for today?" Stephany asked Theodore.

"I haven't made any."

"I'm thinking about going to the city and do some shopping. Do you want to go with me?"

"No. Don't feel like it, although I have to get a souvenir to take back for Jasmine."

"So. Let's go shopping and get it!" Stephany proposed. "I hope you're thinking of going back to St. Lawrence Gap today? the place is only alive at night."

"I know. We should stay here. Monica wants everyone to be here for the official opening of the hotel, and if you go to the city, you may not make it back here in time for the ceremony," Theodore warned.

"Okay. We'll go to the city another day," Stephany agreed.

"Let's have breakfast and then go to the beach," Theodore recommended.

Sherwin A Goodman

Sitting next to Norma in the passenger seat of her BMW SUV on their way to the hotel ceremony, was Jennifer feeling a little lonely with no male escort for either her or her sister Norma.

Jennifer's Nissan pathfinder was in the garage for servicing and won't be ready until the next day.

"Here we are, two unattached sisters," Norma said as she looked over at Jennifer. Then both started laughing.

"What a pair we are," Jennifer exclaimed.

"Our dad asked me a few days ago when he visited the store, when am I going to get married and give him some grandkids," Norma sighed with a schug.

"What did you say to him?"

"I told dad when I find the right guy, I'm going to give him more grandkids than he can handle," Norma replied with a chuckle.

"Is dad coming to the function today?"

"Yes. Monica told me to make sure and bring him."

Joseph closed his car dealership office early on Friday. He picked his girlfriend Marcia at the hairdresser's salon on his way home from the office.

"Wow," Joseph said when Marcia got into the car. "You should have your hair done like that all the time."

"You like it?"

"Of course I do."

Barbados Heroine

"You should thank the hairdresser! She's the one who recommended that I try this style."

"What time do you want to go to the ceremony?"

"These things rarely start on time. The invitation says we should be there at noon."

"We'll get there when we get there. I'm not rushing."

~ ~ ~

Marva Gittens, on her way home from work, stopped and picked up the take out meal she had order consists of fried fish, rice and potato salad.

Arriving home,she took off her jacket along with her handbag, and toss them on a chair in the living.

Marva then put the food on the table, took a glass, add two blocks of ice and covered them with Glenfiddich 18 years old single malt whisky, took a sip, put the glass down, took up her jacket and hand bag and went into the bedroom.

Marva removed her pants and shirt, put on her Carolina silk animal print long robe, took her cell-phone from the hand bag and headed for the pool in her backyard.

Marva's cell phone.

"Hello," Marva said

"Is that anyway to greet your husband on the phone?" Larry Haynes asked with a chuckle.

"When will you be home? I picked up something to eat on my way home,"Marva excitingly said.

"That's why I'm calling. We stopped in Trinidad, I won't be home until sometime next week."

At that moment the house began to ring.

"Hold on for a minute! The house phone is ringing."

Mara went back into the house and answered the phone.

"Hi Cindy, can I call you back. I'm on my cell talking to the hussy."

"Okay," Cindy replied, talk to you later.

"That was Cindy,"Marva explained to Larry when they connected again.

"What's she up too?"

"I have to call her back after I finish talking with you."

"You girls going out tonight? I know how the two of you like going to Oistins on Friday nights."

"We didn't make any plans. I thought you'd be home tonight, then you and I just relax and stay in."

"I will let you know when we're about to leave Trinidad."

"Okay,take care sweetheart!"

"Will do, see you soon," Larry said with a quaver in his voice.

"I miss you very much."

Barbados Heroine

"I miss you very much too. We'll catch up when I get home," Larry promised before hanging up the phone.

As promise, Marva call Cindy.

"What's going on?" Marva asked when Cindy answered on the first buzz.

"He's not coming home, is he?" Cindy asked.

"No. Not until sometime next week," Marva explained.

"I knew something was wrong by the tone of your voice when you answered the phone earlier."

"I was looking forward so much to seeing him tonight, it's been over two months."

"Another couple of days he'll be home."

"I have to spice things up in our bedroom. Try something we never did before, get out of the old wham, bang thank you ma'am sessions," Marva hinted.

"Girl, they're many things you can do to spice things up,"Cindy said.

"Yes, I know. I'll go online and check for new ideas."

"Now that hubby is not coming home tonight, let's do something."

"I didn't feel like going out tonight, because I thought Larry would be home. What do you have in mind?"

"Everyone is talking about the grand opening of the William's Resort & Casino. The elite is going to be there tonight, let's go!" Cindy stated.

"I'm not in the mood. Plus, Jeremy will be there."

"You still seeing him?"

"Yes. And he knows we won't see each other for awhile because Larry was coming home today, I'm sure he will not go to the reception alone," Marva said.

"I'm coming over to get you in an hour, so get yourself ready, we are going out!"

Monica had also invited the next-door neighbor Jeremy Gordon to the opening of the hotel. He brought his New York mistress to be his date for the big event.

By the afternoon, many of the invited guests had arrived, and the hotel was buzzing with activity.

Monica, Stephany, and Jennifer were going around, making sure everyone was comfortable and seated at the reserved tables.

It impressed her dad Rosevelt the way things were shaping up.

"You did it," he said to Monica when she reached his table with pride in his voice.

"I couldn't do it without you guys giving the support when I needed it, and the other investor," she said.

"That's what family is for," her dad replied. "What about your other investor, Randolph? Is he coming down from England?"

"No. Randolph sent an apology. His team is

playing away games for the next two weeks."

"Okay. Go! Do what you have to do."

"I need you and mom to cut the ribbon.

After the cutting of the ribbon by Rosevelt and Sybil Williams, the Williams Atlantic Shores Resorts and Casino.

Jennifer and her sister Norma appeared in the lobby of the hotel wearing matching shiny gold sequin, short to show off their legs, low-cut to show their tits, and dipping at the back just below their waist not leaving much to the imagination. Monica walked over and greeted them.

"No escorts?" Monica asked raising a brow.

"Of course we have. I'm escorting her and she's escorting me," Jennifer replied, then the three of them start laughing.

"Love the outfits," Monica stated as the sisters spun around giving her a full view of their outfits.

"Where is Stephany and Theodore?" Norma asked.

"They're around. I'll get someone to fetch them for you," Monica said.

"No need to do that, we'll find them," Jennifer said with a shrug.

"I have a few things to check, I'll see the two of you later,"Monica uttered while walking away.

Norma and Jennifer headed for the gaming area, and saw Mark Mayers heading out.

"Hi ladies," Mark stopped and greeted Norma and Jennifer.

"Hi Mark,"Norma said."Did you leave anything for us?"

"I won a few bucks. I'll be back later."

"What were you playing?"Jennifer asked.

"The slots machine. Nice to see you Jenn,"Mark said.

"We'll probably be still here when you return," Norma raised a brow.

"Hope so."

"Will you and Mark get back together now that you're finish with your Trinidadian lover?" Norma asked Jennifer.

"That's never going to happened," Jennifer replied.

Theodore dialed his girlfriend's Jasmine cell phone number. She answered on the first buzz.

"Hi, Theodore," Jasmine said. "How's it going? You enjoying the warm weather?"

"Hey, hun, sure I am. Wishing you were here with me, missing you terribly," Theodore said.

"I miss you too," Jasmine responded with a shrug of her shoulder.

"We are a few hours away from the official opening of the hotel and casino."

"I'm sorry I couldn't be there to celebrate with you and the family."

"I know. I'll be back soon."

"Take care! I'll see you when you get back," Jasmine said before turning off her cell phone.

A few minutes after chatting with Jasmine,

Theodore called his friend Alex Smith in London.

"What's up?" Alex asked after answering the call.

"Not much. I'm checking with you to see what you've been doing since I left," Theodore said.

"I met this girl yesterday. Her name's Helen White. And she's performing in a play in the West End. I have to meet her there tonight at her rehearsal."

"Okay, Mr. Playboy," Theodore said. "Keeping yourself busy."

"Helen has a friend what a knock-out, good looks, and a gorgeous body."

"Married? Is her friend married?" Theodore queried.

"I'm not sure. I'll ask Helen when I see her tonight," Alex promised.

"Okay."

"You interested?" Alex curiously asked.

"We'll talk about that when I return."

"Do you want me to hook you up? If she's not dating anyone."

"Let's wait. What will I do with Jasmine?"

"She's not your wife. At least, not yet anyway."

"I know."

"You thinking about marrying her?" Alex asked.

"No. I'm not ready for marriage."

"Let's wait for your return! Enjoy yourself,"

Alex advised. "I'll talk to Helen about her friend."

Jeremy Gordon and his woman Gabriel King walked from his residence to the hotel.

"This way, Mr. Gordan," said the young lady with a clipboard in her hands. "I'll escort you to your table."

"How much did you invest in this hotel?" Gabriel asked.

"I didn't."

"This magnificent structure built next to you, and you didn't invest any money in it?"

"I don't think they are any investors in this project outside of England. I did a few inquiries and found out that all the investors are from England."

"The family has to know the right people to build a hotel/Casino like this with no investors from here," Gabriel suggested.

"Yeah. I understand there's a rich uncle in Florida, and the family has an extensive business in England. Also, the family is well connected both here and in London. There's another daughter who is the CEO of a magazine in London, England."

"Okay," Gabriel said when the seating host reached the table and pulled their chairs back.

"Here we are, Mr. Gordan," the young lady said.

Chapter 15

The opening of the Williams Atlantic Shores Hotel & Casino was a much-coveted event.

Celebrities jetted in from the other Caribbean Islands, and those invited from England and America were excited to be there for the opening celebration.

Press from the Caribbean Islands were there to cover the opening of the hotel. Magazines from around the globe were also there to cover the event.

Security was a priority for the event. They stationed guards at various places in the hotel/casino.

"What do you think?" Monica asked her sister Stephany when she stepped out of her bedroom in a floor-length Marchesa Notte floral appliqued gown, with a faux-pearl embellished necklace, with circle pearl drop earrings.

"Wow," Stephany said while walking around Monica and taking it all in. "Sis, I've never seen you looking so beautiful."

"You like it? Not too fancy, is it?" Monica asked.

"No, this is your moment. You have to stand out above the rest of the individuals," Stephany advised with a raised brow.

"Thanks, Sis."

"How about a drink?" Stephany said, walking behind the built-in bar in Monica's suite.

"Local for me, rum and coke."

"Coming right up, I'll have the same," Stephany stated while pouring two fingers of rum in each glass, then topping them with coca-cola.

Monica walked out onto the terrace and gazed out at the spectacular view of the Atlantic Ocean while Stephany joined her and handed her the rum and coke mixture.

"Cheers. Sis," Stephany said when they touched glasses.

"Cheers," Monica replied, then continued. "Magnificent site, isn't it?"

"Yes, it is," Stephany agreed.

Barbados Heroine

A tear was trickling down on Monica's cheek.

"What's wrong, Sis? You're crying," Stephany said while looking at Monica's face.

"Nothing is wrong. Everything is perfect. I'm happy I was thinking about Joseph. We had talked about this very moment where we would open our hotel," Monica replied and continued. "Let's take a tour of the gaming area!"

"I Was wondering when you were going and check it out."

"You planning to try your luck?" Monica asked.

"Maybe later tonight, I'll have a go at the slots machine."

"Let's go to my office, then do the tour of the gaming area."

In the office, Monica checked her cell phone. A few missed calls. One of them got her attention. Monica immediately punched in the number for Randolph Channing's phone.

The went to voice mail. Monica received a message that the mail-box was full.

Monica then sent Randolph a WhatsApp message letting him know she had returned his call. The sisters then left the office and proceeded to the casino area.

~ ~ ~

The grand entrance of the Casino was the

perfect place for a party. Marble stone floor with a large variety of color candles in silver holders, neatly placed between the columns that lined the entire area.

As Monica and Stephany entered arm in arm, the sight of it all took their breath away. Monica felt a surge of excitement and happiness as she looked around, seeing that all the hard work of putting an idea into reality was finished. Here it was, a Resort/Casino with the family name highlighted at the front, and she was in charge.

"Astonishing!" Stephany whispered to her sister as people began congratulating her with handshakes, cheek kissing and the only reporting press allowed in there capturing every moment was from Stephany's magazine "B.I.A" the other members of the press covering the event were stationed in the Hotel's lobby.

Monica had a group of competent people working for her, and they were doing a great job. From the security, P.Rs, ushers, each one performed their duties flawlessly.

Monica's parents Rosevelt and Sybil, her uncle Otis and his wife Alice, changed from the outfits they wore to the opening ceremony into something more suitable for the evening festive.

Rosevelt and his brother, accompanied by their wives Sybil and Alice, were on the dance floor shaking their booties to the Calypso music.

Jennifer and her sister Norma were on a

winning streak playing the slots machine.

Their dad George Adams was also at the gaming table trying his luck playing poker.

Theodore was in the company of two guys he'd befriended on his night out on the town, Tom Marshall and Edward Collins. The two young men had recently graduated with degrees in High-Tech Surveillance and High-Tech Security from Concordia University in Montreal, Canada.

Tom and Edward were on their fourth visit to the Island, but the first without their parents.

The head of security, Jeffrey Goddard, approached them at the floor entrance.

"Can I be of service?" he asked.

"No, Jeffrey. We'll be fine," Monica said.

Jeffrey Goddard instructed one of his casually dress security people to shadow Monica and her sister as they tour the gaming area. He didn't want the boss lady to encounter any problems on her tour of the Casino.

The two sisters walked past the gaming tables and video slot machines on their way towards the surveillance room.

During the tour, Jennifer saw her dad sitting at the poker table playing. Theodore and his friends were trying their luck at the roulette table.

The last stop was the surveillance room. The person in charge of that department was Ronald Archer. He went on and explained what the surveillance team does.

Sherwin A Goodman

Theodore woke up to find a naked girl laying next to him in bed. He was also naked. Another girl was laying on the sofa. He couldn't remember inviting his two new buddies or the two girls back to his hotel suite.

But here they were. Theodore's head was pounding. His mouth had a bitter taste, and he didn't remember what time he went to bed.

The house phone in his suite rang.

Theodore reached under the sheet and tried to find his underwear then, answered the phone next to the bed.

"Hello," Theodore said.

"This is Monica. Stephany asks me to check on you. You were to go shopping with her this morning, and when you didn't show up, she went on."

"Jeez," he muttered. "What time is it?"

"It's past twelve," Monica said.

"My head hurts like hell, thumping."

"I'll have the barman send something up to your room that will fix that head of yours," Monica assured him.

"Thanks, Sis," Theodore said.

The girl lying in Theodore's bed stirred.

He looked at her and remembered her name was Christy, and the other girl was Marlene. Both girls were visiting from New York and came to the facilities for a night out.

"Time to get up, Christy," Theodore suggested

with a Shrug.

"Um, oh, hi," she replied. "Good morning, handsome."

"Good afternoon."

"Afternoon?" Christy asked.

"Yes, it's after twelve."

"Marlene, time for us to go!" Christy suggested.

"Okay," Marlene said kindly.

"Is it alright to use your bathroom to freshen up?" Christy asked while looking at Theodore. "Will I see you again? I enjoyed our time together."

"Sure, you can freshen up. And yes we'll see each other again. Then I'll treat everyone with lunch," Theodore said.

Tom Marshall and Edward Collins, Theodore's two buddies, were awake and dressed.

Christy and Marlene went into the bathroom. Tom and Edward had smiles on their faces.

"Okay, tell me all about what happened last night!" Theodore demanded. "Did both of you did Marlene at the same time?"

"Yup, we did," Tom replied.

"A threesome. Wow, how was it?" Theodore inquired.

"Marlene was great. She held nothing back," Edward explained.

"How was Christy?" Tom asked with a raised brow.

"To tell you the truth, I remember little after going to bed."

"This I can tell you, I looked over at you, and she was riding you like there's no tomorrow," Edward chortle.

"When the girls are ready, I'm buying lunch for everyone," Theodore said. "Can't let you leave here on empty stomachs."

"No. It'll be my treat," Tom said. "This is your family's hotel. You treated us very well last night. Time for us to pay you back."

"No objections from me," Theodore said with a shrug.

At twelve-thirty, Jennifer pulled into the hotels' parking lot and parked her Nissan Pathfinder.

She got out carrying two brown paper-bags in her hands and headed for Monica's hotel suite.

Jennifer tap on the door with the front of her shoe. Sybil opened the door.

"Come in! Let me help you with that," Sybil said while taking one of the bags from Jennifer.

"Hi, everyone," Jennifer said when she saw the family sitting around the room.

"Something smells awful nice," Alice Williams said.

"Mom sent over a portion of Saturday's daily special of pudding and souse for you guys," Jennifer explained.

"Nice. I haven't eaten any of that stuff in a

long time," Otis said.

"Mom thought you would enjoy it."

Moments later, Monica joined them in the room.

"Ah, you're here, Jennifer," Monica said.

"Yup. I got here a few minutes ago."

"Auntie sent over my Saturday meal," Monica said kindly.

"She send enough for everyone to have a portion," Jennifer explained.

"We must leave a portion for Stephany and Theodore," Monica instructed.

"Oh, yes," Sybil agreed.

"Where are they?" Jennifer asked.

No one answered, they looked at each other.

"Stephany went to the city on the tour bus to do a little shopping, and Theodore is still in his room," Monica explain.

After having lunch with the family.

"I need to borrow a car," Otis uttered.

"You can use mine, I'll be staying here for a few hours," Jennifer said.

"Where are you going?"Otis wife asked.

"Rosevelt and I are going up to our beach house and come back," Otis explained.

"Okay, be careful out there driving on these small roads," Alice advised.

"I'm not driving, Rosevelt will do the driving, he drives on the same side of the road back in London," Otis replied.

"How long will the two of you be gone?" Sybil asked curiously.

"Don't know," Otis replied with a shrug of his shoulders. "Will give you a call when we reach there, and when we are about to leave."

Rosevelt took the car keys from Jennifer, kissed her, Sybil and Monica then headed for the door and left the room followed by his brother Otis.

Reaching outside, Rosevelt push the remote control button and found Jennifer's vehicle. The brothers' got in and drove away.

A few minutes later, they were on the highway heading to Christ Church.

"What you up too?" Rosevelt asked. "You never mention anything about visiting the house until today."

"Nadia is here," Otis replied.

"Who is Nadia?"

"An old flame of mine."

"Where is she staying?"

"She's staying at a guest house in Christ Church," Otis replied.

"You invited her?" Rosevelt asked.

"I mention that the family was going to Barbados for the opening of the Resort/Casino. I didn't ask her to join me. Nadia knew my wife would be here."

"So, what happens now?" Rosevelt asked.

"That's what I have to find out," Otis stated

with anger in his voice.

"So, we are not going to your house?"

"No. We are going to where Nadia is staying."

Twenty minutes later, Otis and Rosevelt arrived at their destination, got out of the car, and entered the lobby of the guest house.

The brothers went to the receptionist's desk.

"Miss Nadia Gomez, can you let her know that someone is here to see her," Otis requested.

The receptionist picked up the phone and punched the number to Nadia's room. While waiting for a reply, she looked at Otis. "And you are?" The receptionist asked.

"Inform Miss Gomez that Otis is here to see her," Otis replied.

The receptionist hangs up the phone after talking with Nadia.

"You can go up to her room."

"What's the number?" Otis asked.

The receptionist gave the room number to Otis.

"I'll be in the lounge when you're ready," Rosevelt said.

"Don't you want to meet her?" Otis asked.

Rosevelt looked at the receptionist as if asking her advice.

"Come on!" Otis urged. "Never know if you'll get the chance again."

The receptionist nodded her head in approval.

"Let's go," Rosevelt said.

Sherwin A Goodman

When Otis and Rosevelt got to the Suite, Nadia was standing with the door open.

She rushed into Otis's arms and began kissing him. Otis returned the affection.

"Nadia, this is my brother Rosevelt from London," Otis said while taking his hands from around her waist.

"Please to meet you," Nadia stated with an extended right hand. "I heard so much about you."

"All good, I hope," Rosevelt said while shaking her hand.

"Yes, but he forgot to mention how handsome you are," Nadia stated while looking into Rosevelt's eyes.

"It's in the genes," Rosevelt replied with a smile on his face.

"I can hook you up with a friend of mine if you ever come to Florida for a visit."

Nadia Gomez stood five feet, ten inches tall, a Buxom body and auburn hair, brown eyes, and twenty years younger than Otis.

At first sight, her appearance took Rosevelt a few moments to take in, but knowing his brother's desire for women, he smiled to himself.

"I'll leave you two lovebirds alone. Otis, You know where to find me when you're ready," Rosevelt said, then he left the suite.

After eating with his friends, Theodore walked with them out to their rental car.

Tom, Edward, and Marlene got into the car.

Barbados Heroine

Christy stood against the car and pulled Theodore close to her.

"Can I see you tonight?" she asked.

"Sure. I don't see why not. I have nothing planned for tonight."

"I'll rent a vehicle when I get back to the guest house where we're staying and call you later," Christy said.

"Okay," Theodore uttered as Christy kissed him, then got into the car with the others.

"Where's dad and uncle Otis?" Theodore asked when he joined the family.

"They went to Christ church to check on uncle's beach house," Jennifer replied.

"There's a portion of black pudding and Souse for you from your aunt Evelyn," Sybil said with a gesture to the refrigerator.

"Yes. A portion for you and one for Stephany," Jennifer stated.

"Where is Stephany?" Theodore asked.

"Stephany is on the tour bus and won't be back until later this afternoon," Monica said.

Chapter 16

Dark clouds filled the sky over the eastern horizon. The view from the Resort/Casino looking out over the Atlantic ocean was spectacular.

Enormous waves twenty feet or higher and frothy white foam on top go rushing towards the sandy beach.

The rain fell as Tom drove away from the Resort.

"Are you guys going back to the Casino tonight?" Christy asked.

"I don't know about you guys, but after last night, I need to sleep for at least a week," Tom stated.

"Me too," Edward said.

"What about you, Marlene?" Christy queried.

"I had a little too much to drink last night. I'll take it easy tonight and rest," Marlene replied.

"What about you, Christy?" Edward asked.

"I will try to see Theodore tonight," Christy replied with a smirk on her face.

"I saw that," Tom said while watching Christy's face in the rear-view mirror. "Memories of last night?"

"You could say that," Christy responded.

Monica left the family gathering to greet an important visitor to the establishment, none other than the prime minister of the Island.

"I understood you had quite a turnout on your opening yesterday," the prime minister said at the end of the greeting formalities.

"Yes, it was," Monica replied.

"I came to offer you my wishes for success, and to let you know if there's anything you should need, just ask."

"I will if the need ever arises."

"I have another engagement. I made this my first stop because those functions go on and on into the late night," the Prime Minister chuckled as if remembering an episode of enjoyment.

"Thanks for dropping by. It was a pleasure to meet you," Monica said.

"The pleasure is all mine. We must do lunch

or dinner."

"Yes, one day soon."

"Here is the number to my direct line. You won't have to go through the switchboard," the Prime Minister said while handing a card to Monica.

"Okay," Monica replied as she took the card.

"We'll talk again soon," the Prime Minister said as he turned and walked towards his car.

Monica walked with him to his vehicle. The Prime Minister got into the driver's seat.

"I gave my chauffer the evening off. There is no need to have my driver at this gathering."

"Take care!" Monica said.

"I always do," he replied as the engine of the Mercedes came alive.

Monica watched as the Prime Minister drove the car onto the East Coast highway and out of sight, then returned to her office.

Moments later, the phone in her office rang, the display screen shows private Monica was hesitant, then picked up the receiver.

"Hello."

"I'm calling to let you know that you'll have to pay us protection money if you need your business to succeed on this Island," the voice on the other end of the phone suggests.

"Is that right?" Monica asked with coolness in her voice.

"Yeah, that's right," he replied in a cold, harsh,

and decisive voice.

"And how much will be the costs for this protection you are offering?"

"A percentage of what the casino takes in on weekends. We're not interested in your bed/breakfast, only the casino."

"We? who are we?"

"That's no concern of yours."

"I'll like to know who I am about to pay for protection," Monica said. I Have to consult with my partners about this."

"Consult with anyone you want to, you still have to pay."

"Hi, sis," Theodore said as he entered the office.

Monica placed her hand over the phone and motioned to her brother to come closer. As he did, Monica turned the phone so that Theodore could hear the voice on the other end.

There was a click, and the line went dead.

"Who was that?" Theodore asked.

"That was someone trying to extort money from me for protection."

"What! you are joking."

"No, I'm not. The voice said I have to pay for protection if I want to do business on the island."

"Did you inform the person that will not happen?"

"No, I didn't. It's best to find out who that person was and who are the people involved because he mentions the word (we) as in more than one," Monica replied.

'So, what are you planning to do?"

"I'll wait for dad and uncle to return and see what they have to say about it."

"How about attaching an answering machine to the phone?" Theodore suggested.

"The phone came with one already built into it," Monica replied.

"I think the recorder only activates after the phone third ring."

"Isn't there a way to adjust the timer?" Monica asked.

"I'll have a look."

"Do not mention this to anyone until after I've spoken to dad and uncle!"

The time was fast approaching for the Casino/Resort first 2-4-1, and Monica needed to freshen up to make her presence felt with the guests and staff.

Leaving Theodore to fiddle with the phone equipment, Monica left the office and went to her suite.

There's no way she would allow some extortionist to spoil the plans she worked so hard in putting together for the opening of Williams Atlantic Shore Resort & Casino.

First, Monica tried on a beige Dolce & Gabbana dress. Then, she decided it was a little too dressy for a casual happy hour.

Barbados Heroine

After settling for an off-shoulder, tropical print, multicolor, slit dress by Chic-me and matching sneakers by Blastiful.

Monica punched in the number for her dad's cell phone and waited.

"Hello," Rosevelt said after the second buzz.

"Happy hour will start shortly. Will you and uncle be back here in time for it?" Monica asked.

"Of course, we will be there."

"Great, but take your time, don't drive too fast trying to get here on time."

"Don't worry!"

"See you soon," Monica said, then turned off her cell phone.

Rosevelt had forgotten about the happy-hour thing. With everything that was going on, and now, this latest with Otis and his mistress coming to Barbados.

Rosevelt left the bar and went to the front desk.

"Can you dial Miss Gomez's room? I'll like to speak with her," Rosevelt said.

The receptionist did and handed the receiver to Rosevelt after informing Miss Gomez about the reason for the call.

"Can I speak to my brother Otis?"

"Yes. Hole on," Nadia replied.

"Hi, bro. What's up?"

"We have to go back now. I completely forgot about the happy hour this evening."

"Oh, yeah. Monica mentioned something about that yesterday," Otis said.

After explaining to Nadia what was going on at the Resort, Otis left her room and joined his brother.

"What happens now?" Rosevelt asked Otis when they got into the car for the drive back to the Resort.

"I still don't understand what got into her. She's usually a very discreet person and has never caused me any trouble or embarrassment," Otis responded with a disappointing tone in his voice.

"How long is she staying here on the Island?"

"Nadia will try to get a flight to go back home Tomorrow."

"Is she upset?"

"She is a little hurt about the situation. I promise to make it up to her," Otis said.

"She's truly in love with you to be so understanding."

"Yes. Nadia is a beautiful person."

"How long it's been?"

"Many, many years."

Jennifer Adams and her sister Norma Adams entered the lounge at 5.30 pm to attend the Williams Resort & Casino first happy hour. They were ushered to a table where Stephany Williams was sitting.

Jennifer wore short white pants with a multicolor blouse and matching pumps.

"Hey, Jenn," Stephany said when the sisters sat down at the table.

"Hello, Cuz," Jennifer replied.

"Where are the others?" Norma asked.

"Dad and uncle are on their way back from Christ Church. Mother and auntie will be here shortly," Stephany said.

"Who will be the first karaoke performer?" Came the booming voice of the MC over the address system.

"I'll do the honor of being the first karaoke performer at this resort," came the voice of a young lady sitting at the back of the lounge.

"Will you introduce yourself?" the MC said to her as he handed the woman the mike.

"My name is Kitty, and I'm from New York."

The crowd applauded with cheers and whistles.

"What will you sing for us? Kitty?" the MC asked.

"I Can See Clearly Now" by Jimmy Cliff is the song I'm going to sing, Kitty replied.

Theodore and Christy entered the room as Kitty sang. They sat at a table away from where the other family members sat.

"I'm sorry. I shouldn't have come," Christy said. "This is a special time for your family, and here I am butting in."

"No. You're not butting in, and besides, I invited Edward Collins and Tom Marshall,"

Theodore replied.

Moments later, Tom Marshall and Edward Collins joined them.

"Hey, guys," Tom said after the usher sat him and Edward at the table.

"Hi," Theodore said.

"Who is the singer?" Edward asked. "She has a magnificent voice, and her body looks damn good too."

"I don't know her. I think her name is Kitty, and she's from the big apple," Theodore replied.

"I'd love to meet her," Edward stated.

"You're a big boy. You can introduce yourself when she's finished singing," Tom suggests.

"First, I'll have to be sure she's alone. Won't want to cause a scene if she is married or here with someone," Edward said.

"I thought you liked Marlene?" Christy asked.

"No. Tom told me, keep my hands off!"

The four of them smiled and stayed quiet throughout the rest of Kitty's performance.

Otis and Rosevelt arrived back at the Resorts a few minutes after the happy hour had started.

After the cocktail hour, which lasted for two hours, had ended,

Monica took her dad, uncle, and brother to her suite.

"I received a call earlier today from someone demanding that I pay them protection money if I want my business to succeed on the Island,"

Monica stated to Rosevelt and Otis.

"What?" Rosevelt shouted.

"You're joking," Otis said.

"No Joke, uncle," Monica replied.

"Who was it?" Otis asked.

"I don't know," Monica said. "How did you make out with the phone, Theodore?"

"It's a built-in answering system, so I called a friend. He will be here tomorrow, and he knows what to do," Theodore responded.

"You didn't mention the call I received?" Monica asked.

"No, I didn't."

"I'll have someone here in a couple of days to fix this," Otis said, then got up from his seat. "Be back shortly."

"Where's uncle going?" Theodore asked.

"Otis will call Florida. He has friends that specialize in the extortion racket," Rosevelt explained to his son.

"Should we inform the rest of the family about this?" Monica asked.

"No, not yet," Rosevelt replied.

"You know, The Prime Minister stopped here on the way to a party given in his honor and said I can call upon him if I ever needed help with anything," Monica said.

"He did? Wow, sis, moving on up," Theodore said teasingly, with a smile on his face.

Otis rejoined them. "It's done. My man will be

on the first available flight he can get out of Florida."

"Okay, I'll have a suite ready for him," Monica said.

"He advised you should stop the receptionist from transferring calls to your private office and get a new cell phone number," Otis said to Monica.

"Okay, I will do that right away."

"Toby might be here sometime tomorrow," Otis said. "I need a drink."

"I'll have a bottle of champagne brought to the room," Monica said.

"Include a Banks beer, no champagne for me," Theodore stated.

"What time is your friend coming tomorrow, Theodore?" Monica questioned her brother.

"He only said in the morning and didn't mention the time," Theodore replied.

Chapter 17

Toby De Leon was born and grew up on the south side of Chicago. His large physic made him a favorite with the local guys. Standing at six feet seven inches tall, broad shoulders and muscular. DeLeon became a member of the neighborhood gang, looking to make things good for his firstborn son. Toby took the advice of his uncle and joined the army.

After his tour of duty ended, Toby took a course in surveillance and then started his own company. Otis and Toby became friends after they first met when Otis encountered a problem at his place of business.

The two men have remained very close over the years. Now, with this attempting extortion in Otis's family business, Toby will do what has to be done and fix it.

Late Monday afternoon, Toby DeLeon got off the plane and passed through customs at Sir Grantley Adams International Airport in Barbados. Waiting for him at the arrival gate were Otis and Rosevelt. The two friends greeted each other.

"Toby, this is my brother Rosevelt," Otis introduces the men as he takes the one piece of luggage from Toby and puts it in the vehicle's trunk.

The three men got into the car, Rosevelt sat behind the wheel, Otis sat in the back seat with Toby.

"Do you have any idea who the asswipe is that's trying to hustle your family for cash?" Toby asked.

"None what-so-ever," Otis replied.

"How was the attempt made?"

"With a phone call."

"How many times did the person called?" Toby asked.

"Just once. My niece took the call. She can explain the event to you much better than I can."

"Okay. How you've been since we last chatted?" Toby asked.

"I'm good. Nadia is here on the island."

"Oh. What is Nadia doing here?"

"I'm surprised as you and my brother were when we first learn she was on the island."

"Where is she staying? Not at the Resort, I hope."

"No. Nadia is staying at a guest house in Christ Church," Otis replied.

"Okay."

"That reminds me. The choice is yours. You can stay at the Resort or my beach house," Otis stated.

"I think it'll be better if I stay close to your niece," Toby said.

"That's what I think also," Rosevelt said.

"Agreed," Otis implied.

On Monday, Monica instructed the receptionist not to put through any calls to her private office.

That Monday morning, Theodore's friend Edward Collins installed a recording machine on the phone extension in Monica's office.

With a few suggestions from Toby DeLeon, by mid-afternoon. Monica instructed the front desk that she was ready to receive calls in her office again.

"How much do I owe you for the work?" Monica asked Edward.

"The material cost a little over two hundred, nothing for the labor. I was glad to help," Edward replied. "And I hope everything goes well."

"Thank you so much," Monica said as Theodore and Edward left the office.

"What do you think about letting the rest of the family know what's going on?" Monica asked Toby.

"I don't see the need to spoil this special moment in your family's life."

"What if mom and auntie ask about you?" Monica queried.

"Leave that to your uncle Otis. He will explain to them who I am and what I'm doing here."

"Yes. That'll be best," Monica agreed.

Toby DeLeon and Monica stayed in her office. Toby instructed Monica on what to say to the caller, but that call never came that afternoon.

"Are you positive Nadia is going to leave on the first flight she can get back to Miami?" Rosevelt asked Otis.

"I have no reason not to believe her," Otis stated. "Nadia will let me know when she gets a flight."

"Sybil thought it was strange the way you suddenly went to the beach house and didn't take them along," Rosevelt said.

"What did you say to her?" Otis asked.

"I told her you wanted to check it because Monica hadn't been there in a while."

"Okay. I'll say the same to Alice if she asks."

Now, the family prepared for their trips back to England and the USA. Otis stays in Barbados for a few more days.

Tuesday afternoon, the extortionist made the call to Monica.

Monica answered the call on the second buzz. "Hello."

"You will put 1000 Barbados dollars in a large brown envelope and drop it off by the second bus stop away from your Resort!" the caller instructed. "Someone will watch, so, no funny stuff."

Toby gestured to Monica with his hand to keep the caller on the line.

"What time do you want me to drop the money off?" Monica asked.

"In thirty minutes," the caller instructed.

"If another person picks up the envelope and you don't get it, what happens?" Monica inquired.

"Don't worry about that. The right people will get the money."

The man hung up after giving the instructions. Monica then called her uncle to the office.

"Find all the small bills you can," Toby said to Monica. "We have a surprise for him."

"What's up?" Otis asked when he entered the office.

"We just had a phone call with instructions on where to take the money," Monica said.

"I recorded the phone message. Let's listen to the playback!" Toby suggested.

Toby, Otis, and Monica listened to the recording.

"Did you hear it?" Toby asked.

"Yup," Otis replied.

"Hear what?" Monica asked.

"There's chatter in the background like someone is typing," Otis said.

"The call came from an office phone," Toby said. "He was smart enough not to use a cell phone."

"What is your plan?" Otis asked.

"I will put a tiny device so I can track the money," Toby said.

"What if the person takes the money and dumps the envelope?" Monica asked.

"Let's hope that doesn't happen, and the person drives away from the pickup carrying the envelope so I can get a signal to track," Toby said.

After Monica took the money and left it at the pickup point, minutes later, someone riding a motorcycle picked up the envelope and rode away without checking the contents.

Monica went back to the Resort, leaving her uncle and Toby to follow the money.

Toby and Otis track the envelope to the District "F" Police Station in Blackman's St. Joseph.

Otis parked the car and watched as a man came out of the station house and shook hands with the rider who handed him the envelope.

Toby snapped a few pictures of the man from the station and the rider who continued wearing the helmet.

"Get a few close-up photos of the man from the station!" Otis suggests to Toby.

"Yup. On it."

"We wait for him to leave and see where he goes," Otis said.

"God damn cop? Crooked son-of-a-bitch," Toby stated.

"Looks that way, doesn't it?"

"Well, he fucked with the wrong people this time. His extortion days are limited."

When the man from the Police Station came out and got into his car, Toby copied the license plate and the make of the vehicle, as the man drove away, Otis followed him.

Toby and Otis return to the Resort later that night. They explained to Monica what had taken place. Monica thanked Toby for his assistants in handling the matter with the extortionist.

A few days later, Otis, along with his wife Alice and Toby, boarded an American Airlines flight and went back to Florida.

Two weeks later, they found a man's body in the wooded area of Farley Hill.

The body was so decomposed. It took an autopsy to help identify the remains of Sergeant Timothy Blackett, and they proved they tortured him to death.

They had stationed Blackett at the District "F" Police Station in St. Joseph at the time of the incident.

That same week, the body of Timothy Blackett's younger brother was discovered down a rocky cliff tangled in the trees.

~ ~ ~

If anyone else was involved with Sergeant Timothy Blackett protection scheme, no one will ever know.

Monica received no more phone calls about paying protection money.

~ ~ ~

The area known to locals as The East Coast Road became a high commodity, as business owners saw a rise of 30% after the opening of Williams Atlantic Shores Resorts & Casino.

In April the following year, Williams Atlantic Shores Resorts & Casino held its first poker tournament just before the start of the (WPT) World Poker Tour.

High roller poker players from around the world descended on the Island of Barbados to try their luck in the first Caribbean poker tournament of its kind.

Monica did her home work on the players and welcomed all of them with her charm and gracefulness.

Barbados Heroine

Sherwin A Goodman

Other books By Sherwin A Goodman

Rick Drago In The Tropics
David Trent
The Caribbean Assassin
Susan & friends
Rick Drago 2 The Missing Prototype
Crosstown

Poetry: Structures Of In-Elegance